The school cafeteria was already crowded when Cindy came in, looking for Grant and Duffy and the others. As she searched through the crowd, she spotted Mollie sitting with a couple of her girlfriends and Chuck. Mollie had both elbows on the table, talking animatedly to Chuck. He squirmed a little uncomfortably under the barrage of Mollie's energetic and devoted attentions, while the two girls with them were talking to each other, turned pointedly away from their table-mates.

Cindy grinned sympathetically, wondering what was going through Chuck's mind. Maybe she should try to rescue him from Mollie, who appeared to be moving full steam ahead. And from the adoring look in Mollie's eyes, Cindy would bet her new surfboard that her baby sister was developing a queen-sized crush on the boy next door.

The SISTERS Series
by Jennifer Cole
Published by Fawcett Girls Only Books:

Other titles in the Girls Only series
available upon request

SISTERS

THE BOY NEXT DOOR

Jennifer Cole

FAWCETT GIRLS ONLY • NEW YORK

RLI: $\dfrac{\text{VL 5 \& up}}{\text{IL 6 \& up}}$

A Fawcett Girls Only Book
Published by Ballantine Books
Copyright © 1988 by Cloverdale Press, Inc.

Library of Congress Catalog Card Number: 88-91157

ISBN 0-449-13497-0

Manufactured in the United States of America

First Edition: December 1988

Chapter 1

*A*s far as Mollie Lewis *was concerned, there* were good weeks and bad weeks—and this had definitely been one of the good weeks! The weather was Santa Barbara sunny, her friends at school had been especially entertaining, and—to top it all off—the cute boy who sat across from her in English class had been all smiles!

"Hey, look, Sarah," Mollie said as the two girls rounded the corner on their bikes after school, "it's a moving truck. We've got new neighbors!"

Mollie and her friend Sarah coasted to a stop at the curb in front of the Lewis house and looked at the yellow Mayflower van parked in the driveway of the vacant house next door.

"I hope they have kids," Mollie remarked, pulling her wavy blond hair off her shoulders to cool down. "This neighborhood needs a little more life."

"Kids?" Sarah asked incredulously, her eyes widening. "A little more *life*? With two sisters, two cats, and a dog that's big enough to pass for the

1

Jolly Green Giant, you hope the neighbors have *kids*?" She shook her head. "You've got to be out of your gourd, Mol."

At just that moment, Mollie's older sister Cindy walked down the drive with her surfboard balanced on her head. Her Walkman was plugged into her ears, and the family dog Winston, a huge black Newfoundland, cantered joyfully at her heels. She wore a floppy T-shirt over her bathing suit, and there was a white smear of sunblock on her nose. Cindy's boyfriend Grant MacPhearson pulled his Trans Am up in front of the house, and Cindy attached the surfboard to the rack on the roof of the car, then she and Winston crowded in and Grant took off.

"You forget," Mollie observed with a grin, "that with Nicole away at college, the Lewis girls are down from three to two. And you've got to admit that *does* take a little of the spark out of things."

"Spark, ha!" Sarah snorted. "It's been my opinion that you and Cindy, even minus Nicole, generate enough electricity to light up all of Cabrillo Boulevard on a foggy night."

But Mollie wasn't listening. She was watching the movers as they wrestled a big green table out of the truck. "Hey, look!" she exclaimed excitedly. "It's a pool table!"

Sarah looked. "Yeah," she said, "and there's a ten-speed bike parked out in front of the garage." She leaned forward, squinting. "And isn't that a stereo they're carrying into the house?"

"Brilliant observation, Watson!" Mollie snapped her fingers. "And where there's a stereo, a pool table, and a ten-speed bike, there's got to be at least one kid, right?"

Sarah nodded. "Right," she said, grinning. "I only hope he—or she, as the case may be—is ready for you." She put one foot on her bike pedal.

"Ready for me?" Mollie asked innocently. "What do you mean?"

Sarah shook her head. "Never mind. Say, do you want to go to the mall tomorrow? There's a bathing suit sale."

"Yeah, sure," Mollie answered, still watching, preoccupied, as the movers unloaded what looked like weight-lifting equipment. It *was* nice that somebody was moving into the empty house, she thought, as Sarah waved and pedaled away.

Just then a boy came out of the front door and began to haul the weight-lifting equipment into the garage. Mollie watched, noting that he moved with an easy, athletic grace. And he was *cute*, really cute, with sandy hair and big shoulders. He looked up, saw Mollie, and waved. She waved back, and then, because she didn't want him to think she was spying, she began to pedal her bike up the drive.

In front of the garage, she turned and stared thoughtfully through the hedge for a few minutes. The boy disappeared into the garage, came out and got something, and then disappeared again. Maybe it would be a good idea to go over and say hello. But it wouldn't hurt to brush her hair first and put on just a dab more lipstick. And while she was at it, she might as well change into shorts—white ones, maybe—and her new blue T-shirt.

A few minutes later, Mollie was walking up the drive of the house next door. The boy was hoisting the weight-lifting equipment into a stand in the garage.

"Hi," Mollie said with a friendly smile that she hoped masked the nervousness she always felt when she met a new guy. Especially a *cute* new guy. "I'm Mollie Lewis. Your next-door neighbor."

The boy turned toward her. "Hi," he said with a grin that showed just the hint of a dimple in each cheek. "I'm Chuck Travis."

Mollie gulped. His eyes were green, a deep, improbable, delightful green. And there were little laugh crinkles at the corners, and his sandy hair curled at the nape of his neck. "Wel ... welcome," she managed, steadying herself. Chuck Travis was the *cutest* boy she'd ever seen. What a break having someone like him move in next door! She steadied herself. "I ... I hope you're getting settled in okay."

"It's hard to tell," Chuck answered with a wry look. He gazed around the garage. "There are so many boxes that I haven't been able to find my mother yet. We'll probably have to settle for a can of soup for supper—if we can find a can opener." He grinned infectiously and Mollie giggled, relaxing. Under the charm of his friendly smile, her butterfly tummy was beginning to settle down. He pulled out a box and opened it, taking out a pair of roller skates. "Do you go to Vista High or to Westside?" he asked.

Mollie replied, "Vista. You?"

"Yeah, me, too," he said. "I'm a junior."

Mollie tried to suppress a sudden surge of delight.

Chuck glanced over his shoulder at her. "Hey, listen, maybe you wouldn't mind taking some time on Monday to show me around—you know, the office, the classrooms, that kind of stuff. I have the feeling that it's going to be a lot different from my old school back in Oregon. We lived in a pretty small town—nothing like Santa Barbara."

"I'd be *glad* to show you around," Mollie bubbled enthusiastically. She got an instant flash of walking down the hall with Chuck, waving and smiling at all her friends. They would all shower her with envious glances and begin to whisper behind their hands, wondering who the handsome new guy was. "And there's a lot to see in Santa Barbara, too," she added enthusiastically. "I mean, there's the beach and the ocean and the old mission and—"

"Hey, sounds terrific," Chuck said. Somebody called from inside the house, and he half turned. "Guess I'm being summoned," he said. "I've got to go—my mom's pretty frazzled and she needs all the help she can get. Thanks for coming over."

"Sure," Mollie said breathlessly. "See you later." She almost skipped back through the hedge, her blond hair bouncing on her shoulders. How neat that her new neighbor was so friendly and nice! Suddenly the already terrific week took on more sparkle and shine, and the weekend ahead positively gleamed.

Back at home in the spacious kitchen, Mollie opened the refrigerator and took out the milk.

There was a note on the refrigerator door from her mother that read: "Catering an afternoon party. Dinner at seven."

Mollie grabbed an apple and some cookies, poured herself a glass of milk, and took her snack to the round oak table. Her mother ran a catering service called Movable Feasts and she sometimes had to cater parties in the afternoon. But the family always managed to have dinner together, even if it was only leftovers from some posh party. She thought of Chuck again with a sharp twinge of sympathy. They'd probably be having soup, he'd said—*if* they could find the can opener.

Then suddenly a thought struck Mollie—a very exciting thought. *She* could cook dinner and take it over to the Travises so that they wouldn't have to eat boring canned soup! Something really elegant and impressive. Something that would make the Travises feel that they had neighbors who really cared about them. A creamy lobster bisque, maybe, with a Caesar salad, chicken Kiev, baby carrots and peas, and lemon sherbet for dessert— all done up in a basket with a snowy cloth and a tiny bouquet of flowers.

Mollie smiled happily as she pictured herself delivering the basket to the Travises and accepting their profuse thanks. And, of course, Chuck would walk her back across the lawn, thanking her all over again. Yes, it was a great idea!

But the smile was quickly followed by a dark frown. When she began to think about the actual preparation of the dinner, Mollie had to admit that there was one small but very vital flaw in her plan. She couldn't cook. She'd already found that out. Once she'd tried to scramble some eggs for breakfast and nearly set the house on fire. If only Nicole weren't away at college! She could cook like an expert, especially gourmet French cuisine. And Cindy's spaghetti sauce was kind of runny but pretty okay, but she wasn't home, either. Cindy was always surfing!

So it was no use dreaming. Salad she could, maybe manage all by herself, if she could find a head of lettuce and some mayonnaise in the refrigerator, and she could always buy some sherbert at the store. But forget the lobster bisque and the chicken Kiev—they were out of the question without Nicole to give her a hand.

Mollie heaved a heavy sigh of disappointment. She'd have to give up the idea of a helpful, neighborly, elegant dinner. And Chuck and his parents would just have to eat soup.

Unless . . .

Mollie was suddenly struck by another idea, even more exciting that the first. She gulped down the rest of her milk, stuffed the last of the apple into her mouth, and ran to the garage to get her bike. Pedaling as fast as she could, she covered the few blocks to her mother's catering shop, parked the bike in the back, and dashed through the door.

Amanda, one of her mother's assistants, was carving the last slices of a juicy-looking prime rib. "Hi, Mollie," she said.

"Hi," Mollie replied breathlessly. "Where's Mom?"

Amanda put down the knife and wiped her hands on her apron. "At the country club finishing up the party. Did you come for the dinner?"

Mollie did a double take. She had thought she'd have to beg, the way she usually did when she wanted a snack or something from Amanda. "As a matter of fact," she said excitedly, "I did. Is there something I can take?"

"You're just in time," Amanda said. "I made up some boxes a few minutes ago. They're over there on the counter. But don't drop them on your way home," she cautioned. "It's the very last bit of food in the place. The party cleaned us out."

"Oh, I won't," Mollie promised breathlessly. She counted. There were four boxes. Good—that meant that Chuck could have seconds. Curious, she opened the top one. What luck! It wasn't chicken Kiev; it was something even *more* enticing. It was Mollie's favorite: thick, fragrant slices of prime rib, with tiny parslied new potatoes. And to round off the dinner there were a cup of cold, rich vichyssoise and a bowl of her mother's famous spinach salad. There was even a big fat piece of tasty carrot cake—Cindy's favorite—for dessert.

Mollie stared hungrily at the cake. Maybe she could just sneak a tiny bit. But then she made a determined face. No, this was the Travises' dinner and she wouldn't touch it, not even a crumb. And anyway, there were the calories to think about. She closed the top, feeling virtuous.

"The rib and potatoes can go in the microwave to warm them up," Amanda told her as she picked up the boxes.

"Flowers?" Mollie asked. "Do you suppose there are any flowers I could take?"

"Sure," Amanda said. "Look in the cooler. There

ought to be some daisies and carnations left over from the wedding we catered yesterday."

Mollie said good-bye to Amanda and then, carefully balancing the boxes on her handlebars, she headed home. There, she found a large basket that Grandma Lewis had given them for Christmas with grapefruit in it. After that, she dug through the closet until she found one of her mother's white linen napkins. She arranged the food in the basket and covered it with the cloth. Then she tied the daisies and carnations in little bunches on the handle with some blue velvet ribbon that she found hanging over Cindy's mirror. She stepped back to admire her handiwork. It looked fantastic— like a picture of a romantic picnic that she'd seen in *Seventeen*. She was certain that the Travises would be as impressed as she was. Not even her sister Nicole could have done a better job.

On her way out the door with the basket, Mollie looked down at her white shorts. Somehow her outfit didn't quite fit the friendly, helpful neighbor image she wanted to project. Certainly Nicole would have worn something different. She hurried upstairs and changed again, this time into a plaid skirt and a demure white blouse that made her look more grown-up and sedate. She smoothed her blond hair into a ponytail and tied it with a red ribbon. Then, inspired by her new look, she fished through the pile of shoes on her closet floor until she found an old pair of black flats, which she put on with a pair of knee-length white socks. Glancing into the mirror, she gave herself a modest smile of approval. She looked neat and tidy and very feminine. It was exactly the right look for her new project: Project Good Neighbor.

Mrs. Travis answered Mollie's knock. She was an attractive woman with trim dark hair and Chuck's green eyes. But right now she looked weary and harried.

"Hi," Mollie said, surreptitiously looking over Mrs. Travis's shoulder, hoping to see Chuck coming down the hall. "I'm Mollie Lewis from next door," she continued. "Your new neighbor."

"Oh, yes," Mrs. Travis said, and nodded. "I think Chuck mentioned meeting you."

Mollie gave Mrs. Travis a warm, sympathetic smile and held out the basket. "Chuck said you might have to have soup for supper, so I've brought you something for dinner. It's from my mother's catering shop," she added hastily, not wanting Mrs. Travis to think that she'd actually done the cooking herself.

Mrs. Travis looked startled. "Soup?" she asked. Then, with a little smile, she recovered herself. "Why, how very thoughtful of you, Mollie," she said, taking the basket. She lifted up the white cloth to peek inside. "Mmmm. Whatever it is, it smells simply delicious. And that carrot cake looks marvelous."

"The prime rib and the potatoes can go in the microwave," Mollie said helpfully, repeating Amanda's instructions. "To warm them up if they're cold."

Mrs. Travis shook her head and gazed with a wondering look at the little bunches of flowers tied with Cindy's blue ribbon. "I can't tell you how touched I am. If the other neighbors are as friendly as you are, I'm sure we're going to love living here."

Mollie smiled her best smile. "I can guess what a hassle it is to move," she said. "Listen, I hope you'll let me know if there's anything else I can do to help—anything at all." She craned her neck once more looking for Chuck, but he was nowhere in sight.

Inside, the phone rang. "Oh, there's the phone," Mrs. Travis said distractedly, beginning to close the door. "Thanks *so* much, Mollie. You're a good neighbor."

"You're welcome," Mollie said, resisting the desire to curtsy. As she went down the driveway, her smile broadened. Project Good Neighbor had obviously been a smashing success, even if Chuck hadn't been around to walk her to the street. Nicole would have been so *proud* of her! Her mother would be proud, too, when she found out what Mollie had done.

Now, let's see, she thought eagerly, glowing with the warm, virtuous feeling that comes from having done something nice. What can I plan for Project Good Neighbor tomorrow?

Chapter 2

*I*t was nearly six-thirty when Cindy said good-bye to Grant and climbed over Winston to get out of the Trans Am. The new boy next door—the one she'd seen earlier that afternoon—waved at her from in front of his garage and she waved back. Even from a distance, she thought, you could tell that he was cute—a hunk, as Mollie would say. But not as cute as Grant, of course. *Nobody* was as cute as Grant.

Cindy frowned a little as she shouldered her surfboard and followed Winston up the sidewalk, but it wasn't because of anything that had happened that afternoon at the beach. The afternoon had been great as usual, full of warm sun and the long, steady rollers that were a surfer's delight. And it didn't have anything to do with Grant, because their relationship felt warmer and nicer than ever.

No, the frown was about something that had happened yesterday, something that she'd been turning over and over in her mind since then. It was a remark that her new swim coach, Coach Sweeney, had made when she was late for prac-tice. For the past couple of weeks, Coach Sweeney had been subbing for Coach Lawford, who was out having back surgery. Cindy had been late to practice for a very good reason: the class election committee meeting had taken longer than it was supposed to, and afterward she'd had to talk to Mrs. Norris, the journalism teacher, about the article she was writing on last week's swimming meet. It was Cindy's first article and she wanted it to be good.

But Coach Sweeney hadn't been in the mood to hear *why* she was late. She had scowled sternly and said, "You've got too many distractions in your life, Lewis. If you don't settle down and keep your mind on your swimming, you're in for trouble."

Too many distractions? How could you be a junior in high school and *not* have distractions in your life? She frowned again, a little more angrily. She was beginning to get the feeling that if Coach Sweeney had her way, there wouldn't be anything in her life *but* the swim team!

With a sigh, Cindy hoisted her surfboard onto the rack her father had built in the garage. It was too bad that Nicole wasn't here to help her sort this out. Of course, she could always give her sister a call at Briarwood College, but that was all the way across the country on the East Coast. After they'd gotten last month's phone bill, her father had hit the ceiling and made a new rule about paying for your own calls out of your al-lowance. She sighed again. No matter how helpful

Nicole was, or how much she missed their long conversations, talking to her would have to wait.

Cindy put Winston out in the backyard so that he could run around and dry his shaggy black fur, still slightly damp from romping in the surf. Then he headed for the kitchen, where she could hear her mother talking on the phone.

"I'm home," she announced, coming into the kitchen. She wrinkled her nose and sniffed hungrily. Surfing always gave her a roaring appetite. But tonight she couldn't smell anything. She opened the oven door and looked in. It was empty. "What's for dinner?" she asked as her mother put down the phone and turned around.

Laura Lewis was a pretty, petite woman, vivacious like Mollie and fired with Cindy's enormous energy. "Prime rib," she said, ticking off the items on her fingers. "With parslied potatoes, spinach salad, and vichyssoise." She smiled at Cindy. "Oh, yes—and carrot cake."

"Terrific." Cindy let out an anticipatory sigh, closed the door of the empty oven, and sat down at the kitchen table, hitching up her T-shirt and stretching out her tanned, athletic legs. "Sounds like leftovers from somebody's retirement dinner." Cinders came out from under the table and began to rub against Cindy's legs, purring loudly.

"Right the first time," Mrs. Lewis said, laughing, too. "Give that girl a medal." She ruffled her daughter's short-cropped blond hair affectionately. "I was so busy at the country club this afternoon that I didn't have time to think about *our* dinner, so I asked Amanda to make up some boxes for us. I planned to bring them home myself, but when I phoned the shop, Amanda said that Mollie had already picked them up. Wasn't that nice of her?" She went to the refrigerator and opened the door, peering inside. "Now, all I have to do is find what she did with those boxes, and we'll have dinner in a jiffy."

Just then Mollie walked into the kitchen. Cindy noticed that she was wearing the starry-eyed look that usually meant trouble. She was also wearing a strange-looking outfit—a red plaid skirt and a long-sleeved white blouse buttoned up to the collar—that made her look like a refugee from a prep school.

"Hi, shrimp," Cindy said. "What's up? What's that you're wearing?"

"Did you know," Mollie said dreamily, still thinking about how pleased Mrs. Travis had been with the basket, "that we have new neighbors?"

Cindy nodded. "Yeah," she said, taking an apple from the wooden bowl on the table. She sat back and took a big bite. "I saw the moving truck. Looks like there's a guy in the family, huh? And kind of cute at that."

Mrs. Lewis straightened up and closed the refrigerator door. "Mollie, what did you do with our dinner?" she asked. "I can't find it."

"Our dinner?" Mollie repeated blankly. "Was I supposed to do something with our dinner?"

Cindy smothered a giggle. When Mollie was obsessed with an idea, the way she obviously was at the moment, you might as well forget asking her to do anything. Her sister was a sweet kid, but at times she could be a real fluff-brain, no two ways about it. She always took things to the extreme.

Mrs. Lewis tapped her foot impatiently. "Amanda said that you picked up the four boxes I was saving for our dinner and ..."

There was a long silence as Mollie stared disbelievingly at her mother. "You mean, those dinners were for *us*?" she asked finally in a very small voice.

Her mother made a strangling sound. "Yes, of course they're for us," she said tersely. "Who else? Come on, Mollie, where did you put them? Dad will be home any minute, and he'll be starving."

"Yeah, Mollie," Cindy chimed in, thinking of the carrot cake. "Come on, give. Where did you stash our dinner?"

Mollie cleared her throat. "Well, the truth is ... I mean, I ..." She stopped and threw her mother a stricken look. "I gave it away," she whimpered helplessly.

Cindy's eyes widened. Her younger sister had done some pretty dippy things in the past, but this had to be one of the dippiest. "You gave it away?" she asked, shaking her head. "Awe-*some*."

"You gave it away?" Mrs. Lewis echoed incredulously. "For heaven's sake, Mollie Lewis, who did you give it to?"

"Gave what away?" Mr. Lewis asked cheerfully as he entered the kitchen. He looked around and sniffed. "I'm hungry enough to eat french-fried seaweed. What's for dinner?"

"But I didn't know it was *our* dinner," Mollie wailed dramatically, collapsing in a heap on a chair. "I thought the boxes were extras, and I gave them to the people next door." She looked at her family, enormous tears beginning to gather in the corners of her big blue eyes. "I just wanted to be helpful!"

"The people next door?" Mrs. Lewis asked even more incredulously.

Cindy stared at her sister. "You mean, the people who are moving in?" she asked. "What did you do a stupid thing like that for?"

"What did Mollie give to the people next door?" Mr. Lewis asked in a puzzled voice, looking from one to the other.

"Our dinner!" Cindy and her mother said in unison.

There was another long silence, broken only by the sound of Mollie's loud sniffling.

"Our dinner?" Mr. Lewis said at last. He stared at Mollie for a minute and then turned to his wife. "What was it?" he asked sadly. "Our dinner, I mean. What were we having?"

"Prime rib," Mrs. Lewis said. "With parslied potatoes and vichyssoise."

"And carrot cake," Cindy added, heaving a large sigh.

"Too bad," Mr. Lewis said regretfully. "I *love* parslied potatoes." He gave Mrs. Lewis a hopeful look. "Maybe we could make a fast raid on the shop for some more?"

"I'm sorry," Mrs. Lewis said, shaking her head, "but there *isn't* anymore. We're completely cleaned out."

Mr. Lewis looked disappointed. *"C'est la vie,"*

he muttered, borrowing one of Nicole's favorite French phrases.

Mollie hiccuped and wiped her eyes on the sleeve of her white blouse. "Listen, I didn't *mean* to give our dinner away. I didn't know it was our dinner. I was just trying to be neighborly because Mrs. Travis was so frazzled unpacking boxes and the Travises were going to have soup for dinner."

"Soup," Mrs. Lewis said thoughtfully, going to the big walk-in pantry. "Now there's an idea. Maybe we could have some chicken noodle soup."

For some reason, Mollie looked even more stricken. "Soup?" she asked tearfully. "We're going to have *soup*?"

Suddenly the light dawned and Cindy began to laugh. "I think I know the answer to this mystery," she said, snapping her fingers. "There's a *boy*."

Mrs. Lewis turned. "A boy?" she asked.

"Just moved in next door." Cindy held her hand up over her head. "Tall, blond, b-i-g shoulders, probably from cross-country skiing. He lifts weights, too. I saw the equipment in the garage. And he waved at me tonight when Grant drove me home. He's really a hunk." She snickered knowingly. "Mollie was probably just trying to impress him."

Mollie threw Cindy an indignant look. "I was *not* trying to impress anybody," she said. "I was just trying to be a good neighbor." She folded her arms across her chest, looking a little sulky. "Nobody else in the neighborhood thought of taking them anything for dinner, and they were going to eat soup. It was up to me. I wanted to be helpful."

Mr. Lewis sighed. "A new boy in the neighborhood," he said with resignation. "It figures." Then he rubbed his hands, brightening a little. "Listen, gang, with all due respect to the cook, I'm not in the mood for chicken noodle soup tonight. I was thinking about egg rolls. How does a Chinese dinner sound to the rest of you?"

"Chinese is great with me," Cindy said, getting up. "I'll go change." She paused in the door and frowned at Mollie. "But it's too bad about the carrot cake. You really blew it this time, kid."

"Chinese will be fine," Mrs. Lewis said, closing the pantry door. She turned to Mollie. "Mollie, it was a very generous impulse that led you to take dinner to our new neighbors, and I think it's wonderful that you thought of their needs. But the next time you're struck by an overwhelming urge to be a good neighbor, will you please check with us? Remember the old saying 'Charity begins at home'?"

Mollie bowed her head meekly, the picture of penitence. "Yes, ma'am," she said.

Cindy couldn't help a loud snicker.

Chapter 3

*"M*om, do we have a map of Santa Barbara?"

Wearing her bright green robe, with her hair still tousled from sleep, Mollie stood at the door of the family room. It was early Saturday morning, and her mother was picking up the popcorn bowls left over from the family's TV watching the night before. Outside the windows, a gray mist filled the air, but it didn't bother Mollie. She knew it would burn away when the sun rose higher in the sky.

"A map?" Mrs. Lewis reached under the sofa for the salt shaker. "Well, let's see. If you look in my desk in the kitchen, you might find one there. And a guidebook, too, I think." She gave Mollie a quizzical look. "What do you want the map for? Are you planning on getting lost?"

"I just wanted to look at it," Mollie said vaguely, rubbing the sleep out of her eyes. She'd awakened just a few minutes ago with a plan already beginning to form in her mind. A plan for Project Good Neighbor that couldn't get her in any kind of trouble. Wouldn't it be helpful if the Travises had a sort of "care package" of items about Santa Barbara? Things like maps and library information and a guide to the Museum of Art and copies of the newspaper—stuff that would help them find their way around and keep them from wasting time when they wanted to go downtown or to the library.

Still thinking about her great idea, Mollie went into the kitchen, where Cindy was sitting at the breakfast table in her pink jogging suit, eating a bowl of cereal and reading her latest copy of *Surfing*. She'd obviously been out for her usual Saturday-morning jog, for her cheeks were almost as pink as her jogging suit and she had a relaxed but energetic look.

"Hi, squirt," she said casually, not looking up from her magazine. "What's up with you this morning?" Sprawled across Cindy's feet, Winston began to beat an unrestrained "good morning" with his black tail.

"Oh, nothing, really," Mollie replied evasively, bending over to pat Winston. She went to her mother's desk in the corner of the kitchen and began to rummage through the papers. In a minute, she found exactly what she was looking for, a Santa Barbara guidebook and a map. The map had seen better days, but it would do the trick.

With a surreptitious glance at her sister, Mollie stuck the map and the guidebook into the pocket of her floppy robe. There was no point in calling Cindy's attention to what she was doing—she'd only have to answer a bunch of questions and wind up getting teased about trying to impress

Chuck. And that wasn't what she was doing at all, she reminded herself virtuously. She was only being helpful to the whole Travis family. She was practicing the principles of neighborliness.

Mollie poured herself a glass of orange juice and sat down at the table across from Cindy, feeling the weight of the contraband guidebook in her pocket.

"So what are you doing today?" she inquired in a bright, friendly way, remembering what her mother had said last night about charity beginning at home. If she was going to go out of her way to be helpful to the neighbors, she ought to carry it one step further and be helpful to her sister as well. Even if she didn't deserve it after the way she'd carried on last night about that stupid carrot cake.

Cindy made a face. "I've got swim practice this morning," she said. "And I'm taking the car, so don't plan on Mom driving you anywhere."

"Swim practice? On Saturday?"

"Yeah," Cindy answered, looking disgruntled. "This substitute coach, Coach Sweeney, says we're getting ragged. We need to work harder."

"If you spend any *more* time in the water," Mollie remarked, "you'll dissolve. Between swimming and surfing and water polo, you're in the water every minute."

"Well, I don't care what Coach Sweeney says," Cindy replied defiantly, "I'm bugging out at noon. Grant and I are taking a bike hike this afternoon to the orchid ranch in Goleta."

"Hey," Mollie said, suddenly struck by a new thought, "that sounds like fun!"

Cindy gave her a sharp look. "Listen, if you're angling for an invitation, shrimp, you'd better go fishing somewhere else. Haven't you got something to do with your friends today? Do you always have to tag along with Grant and me?"

Mollie pulled herself up, offended by Cindy's question. "I certainly do," she said with great dignity. "I have an important project of my own that's going to keep me busy *all* day."

And she did, too. It had just occurred to her that it would be helpful to Chuck if she offered to give him a guided bike tour of Santa Barbara. That way, he would see all the sights and get to know the city.

"Oh, yeah?" Cindy asked. "So, what is this big project of yours?"

Mollie hesitated. She knew how Cindy would tease her if she told her, so she said, "Oh, just a long bike ride. I have to get more exercise," she added in explanation, "if I'm ever going to lose five pounds."

"Yeah, exercise helps," Cindy said in a more kindly voice. She got up and carried her cereal bowl to the sink to rinse it off. "Well, I hope you have a fun day, Mollie-o."

"Oh, I plan to," Mollie said happily, finishing her orange juice. She smiled at Cindy as she stood up, imagining how pleased the Travises were going to be with her care package and thinking how good it felt to be useful to other people. "And if there's anything I can do to help you out," she went on sweetly, "be sure to let me know. Okay?"

As Mollie left the kitchen, she could feel Cindy's startled gaze on the back of her neck.

Cindy pulled on her cap and hurried to catch up with Liz Wright and Maureen Kilmurray as they walked across the concrete deck of Vista High's swimming pool.

"Hey, Cindy," Liz asked, "what's this rumor I hear about you running for class president?"

"Yeah, what about it, Lewis?" Maureen chimed in.

Cindy shrugged a little. "Oh, *that* rumor," she said with a mysterious little smile. "Yeah, I heard it, too."

The fact was that Cindy was only serving on the class election committee—she had no intention of running for president. But if Liz and Maureen wanted to think so, Cindy certainly wasn't going to correct them. Liz, a transfer student and a top-flight athlete, had proven to be Cindy's equal in the pool, while Maureen, who'd chafed at always being second-best to Cindy, had obviously been tickled pink at Cindy's new competition.

Maureen gave her a sideways look. "Think you're going to have time to be president *and* time for the swim team, too?" she asked.

"If I decide to run for president," she said evenly, "I'm sure I'll be able to *make* time."

"You're sure?" Maureen inquired sweetly. "After all, Liz *did* beat you in freestyle twice this week, you know. And Coach Sweeney is really cracking down on us—she insists we can do better."

Cindy's jaw tightened. It was true. Liz had beaten

her—again. But she was trying to keep it from bothering her, from affecting her concentration, and she didn't need Maureen's taunt. And she *really* didn't need the coach ganging up on her, nagging her about how much time she gave to swimming.

At that moment, Coach Sweeney caught up with them. "You two get in your lanes with the others," she said with a motion of her head at Liz and Maureen. "Lewis, I want to talk to you for a minute."

With a meaningful grin, Maureen trotted toward the pool, Liz behind her. Cindy pulled in her breath sharply. She could tell by the look on the coach's face that she had something serious on her mind.

"I've been watching you for the last week or so, Cindy," the coach said as they stepped over to the side of the pool. "It looks to me like your timing is off a little."

"Yeah," Cindy said. She swallowed, her stomach sinking. "A little, maybe. I'm working on it."

"And your timing's off when it comes to getting places, too. You were late to practice twice last week."

Cindy swallowed again. "Yeah, I guess," she said. "But both times it was because—"

But the coach didn't let her finish. "Listen, Lewis," she said sternly, "I know that I'm not your regular coach. But I know that I'm speaking for Coach Lawford when I say that if you expect to stay on the team, you've got to pay more attention to your swimming. As far as I'm concerned, it's a matter of priorities, and the swim team comes first. Not surfing, not water polo, not running for class president—"

"But I'm *not* running for class president!" Cindy exclaimed.

The coach gave her a disbelieving look. "But I just heard you tell Maureen and Liz that you—"

"It's only a rumor," Cindy said desperately. "Honest. I'm not running for anything."

"Well, I still mean what I've said," Coach Sweeney said with a stubborn look. "There's too much going on in your life. You've got to move the team up on your list of priorities. And that's all there is to it! You got that, Lewis?"

"Yes, ma'am," Cindy said glumly. "I've got it."

Below her, in the water, Maureen Kilmurray snickered.

This time, it was Chuck who opened the Travises' front door. His sandy hair was rumpled as if he hadn't combed it yet this morning, and the green T-shirt he was wearing really made his eyes sparkle.

"H-hi, Chuck," Mollie said. She was glad she'd worn shorts again rather than the friendly-neighbor outfit she'd put on yesterday evening. "I've brought you something." She thrust her care package at him. "Well, it's not exactly for you. It's for your whole family, sort of."

"Oh? Another present?" Chuck smiled, and the dimple flashed in his cheek. "That dinner you brought last night was really terrific, Mollie." He looked down at the box in his hands. "Why don't you come in while I open this?"

Mollie took a deep breath. "Oh, yeah. Sure."

Chuck led her to the den in the back of the house and they sat on the sofa while he opened the shoebox Mollie had wrapped in bright paper.

It's not really very much," Mollie said, blushing a little, "just a guidebook and maps and stuff."

"Boy, is my mom going to be glad to see this," Chuck said, holding up a pamphlet entitled "Everything You Need to Know About Your Library." "She was just saying this morning that she had to get a library card first thing." He unfolded another pamphlet. "What's this?"

"Oh, there's some stuff in there about the Carriage Museum and the El Paseo Arcade, in case your mom's into antiques. And there's a brochure about the mission—it costs fifty cents if you want to go in—and another about the fig tree," Mollie explained earnestly.

Chuck seemed to be trying to suppress a smile. "The fig tree?"

"Oh, yes!" Mollie exclaimed, delighted that Chuck was so interested. "You see, we've got the oldest fig tree in the whole, entire United States right here in Santa Barbara."

"I'll bet it's something to see," Chuck said in a marveling tone.

"Oh, it *is*," Mollie said vigorously. "In fact, if you'd like to take a look at it, I'd be glad to show it to you. In fact, I thought—if you wanted to—that we could take a tour—on bikes, of course, all through Santa Barbara." She leaned over and spread out the map, trying to keep from tearing its worn folds. "I've got it all planned out," she announced happily, using her finger as a pointer. "We could bike down to the yacht harbor and look at the boats, and then go out on Stearns Wharf and—"

"Don't forget the fig tree," Chuck said with a grin.

"Oh, yes, the fig tree," Mollie said eagerly. "Absolutely, we don't want to forget the fig tree. It's real close to the wharf. And then we could go past the Historical Museum and the Museum of Art and up Santa Barbara Street to the mission." She gave Chuck an anxious look. "What do you think?"

"Sounds like a great idea to me," Chuck said. "But I'm afraid the movers trashed my bike. They snapped the pedal off. Dad took it to the repair shop this morning so I'll have it to ride to school next week."

"Oh, that's okay," Mollie said hastily. "We've got *tons* of bikes at my house. Nobody's using Nicole's bike. She's my older sister who's away at college," she said as an afterthought.

Chuck thought for a minute. "Okay," he said, "as long as we get started right away and it doesn't take more than a couple of hours. I've got something I have to do later this afternoon."

"Sure!" Mollie exclaimed, delighted. "Let's get the bikes and take off!"

But when she and Chuck got to the garage and pulled Nicole's bike down from the ceiling rack where it was stored, she gave a loud groan. "Oh, *fudge,*" she exclaimed, pounding her fist on the seat in frustration. "The tire's flat. Wouldn't you know it?"

"Listen, that's okay," Chuck replied cheerfully.

"We can make it another time. I've got enough to do to keep me—"

"But we can take Cindy's bike," Mollie interrupted hurriedly, pushing Nicole's to one side. "She's at swim practice this morning, and she doesn't need it until this afternoon." What time had Cindy said that she and Grant were going for their bike hike? Well, it didn't really matter—she and Chuck would be back in a couple of hours, and Cindy wouldn't even have to know she'd borrowed it.

Chuck grinned. "Well, okay," he said. "But I really need to be back by two."

"Oh, we'll be back *long* before then," Mollie told him happily as they wheeled the bikes out of the garage. This was great—it was perfect! Not only was she being a helpful neighbor to somebody who was new to Santa Barbara, but she was going for a bike ride on a beautiful Saturday with a *very* cute guy!

"I know I'm an hour early," Grant said when Cindy opened the front door just before noon, "but the weather's so nice that I thought we might get started." His bike was parked on the sidewalk behind him, and a blue nylon backpack was slung across his shoulders. "Are you ready to go yet?"

Cindy swallowed the last of her grilled-cheese sandwich. "Yeah, you bet I'm ready," she said with a frown.

"What's that supposed to mean?" Grant inquired, raising his eyebrow quizzically as they went through the kitchen.

"It means that I've had an utterly *lousy* morning in the pool and I need a bike ride through the hills to make me feel like a member of the human race again," Cindy told him, opening the garage door. "The coach seems to think that my mind isn't one-track enough," she added gloomily. "She wants me to give up surfing and bike riding and running for president and—"

"I didn't know you were going to run for president," Grant replied, surprised.

"I'm not," Cindy admitted. "But even if I wanted to, I couldn't." She mimicked the coach's stern voice. "Lewis, you've got to move swimming up on your list of priorities."

Grant squeezed her shoulder affectionately. "Now, you just listen to old Dr. MacPhearson, my child," he said. "I prescribe lots of sunshine and ocean breezes and a great afternoon at the orchard ranch. And if that doesn't cure your swimming-coach blues, maybe we can try for dinner at the pizzeria. What do you say?"

"I say, let's get going!" Cindy sighed happily, grateful to Grant for cheering her up. She turned to get her bike. "Hey!" she exclaimed. "Where is it?"

"Where is what?" Grant asked.

"My bike!" Cindy wailed. "I saw it right here this morning when I took out the car. And now it's gone!"

Grant looked around. "You don't suppose it's been stolen, do you?" he asked. "Looks like Mollie's bike is missing, too."

"But there's Nicole's bike," Cindy said, pointing. "It's got a flat tire, but you'd think that wouldn't matter to somebody who wanted to steal it. And there's Dad's outboard and all our skiing equipment. Thieves would take all that stuff, too, wouldn't they?"

Grant scratched his head. "Yeah, I guess they would." He looked up. "Hey, maybe Mollie—"

"Mollie!" Suddenly Cindy remembered what Mollie had said at breakfast about going for a bike ride, and anger flared inside her. "Mollie said she was going for a bike ride, but she wouldn't tell me who she was going with. I'll bet *she* took my bike! And she knew that I was going to be using it this afternoon, too," she added in disgust.

"Well," Grant suggested reasonably, "why don't we take Nicole's bike down to the gas station and pump up the flat. It'll stay up, won't it?"

"I don't know," Cindy muttered. "I guess maybe it will." She scowled, still fuming. "But just wait until I find that deceptive little sneak!"

It was almost three when Mollie and Chuck wheeled the bikes into the garage. "Listen, Chuck," Mollie said unhappily for the third time, "I'm really sorry about what happened. If I'd known that the tour through the mission was going to take a whole hour, I never would have suggested it."

"Forget it, Mollie." Chuck shrugged. "These things happen." He looked at his watch. "Gotta run. I'm late already. Thanks again for a great tour."

Mollie watched him dash down the driveway. It *had* been a great tour, until she'd gotten the bright idea of going through the mission. They'd gotten stuck with a dull, boring guide who'd droned on and on, while Chuck got more and more nervous about the time. As far as Mollie was concerned, it had spoiled the whole day.

She leaned Cindy's bike up against the wall and then, with a puzzled frown, noticed that Nicole's bike was gone—flat tire and all. Who would have taken it? Who . . .

And then, with a sinking stomach, Mollie remembered. *She* had had Cindy's bike, and Cindy and Grant had planned to go for a long ride today.

Oh, wow, she thought miserably. She was really in trouble now.

Chapter 4

"*W*hat's the matter, Cindy?" Mrs. Lewis asked as Cindy flopped down at the breakfast table on Monday morning.

"I *hate* Mondays," Cindy grumped. Under the table, Winston nudged her knee with his cold, wet nose, commiserating. "Mondays are the pits, the absolute pits." Winston made an assenting noise deep in his throat.

"Since when do you hate Monday?" Mollie inquired brightly, bouncing into the kitchen and dropping her books on the table with a loud *thud*. "I thought Monday was your favorite day."

"Have you looked outside?" Cindy sighed. "It's pouring." She glanced at her sister and scowled. "And how come you're all dressed in yellow this morning?" she asked. "You look like a field of daffodils on its way to a party."

Nicole's bike had worked out okay on Saturday, and Mollie had apologized tearfully for taking Cindy's, explaining that she and the new guy next door had decided to take a tour of the mission and got stuck for longer than they'd expected. After hearing all the details, Cindy had accepted Mollie's apology and her offer to take kitchen duty for two nights. But she was still ticked off at her sister for taking her bike without asking permission.

Mollie glanced down at her bright yellow blouse and skirt with a look of dismay. "You don't think I've overdone it, do you?" she asked worriedly. "Maybe I ought to go up and change again. I tried on a red outfit, but it didn't seem—"

"You look just right for a cloudy, rainy day," Mrs. Lewis assured her with a smile. "Don't let Cindy get you down. This morning she's got a different color on her mind."

Looking at Mollie's distressed face, Cindy wished she had held her tongue. The fact that she was in such a deep, dismal funk didn't have anything to do with Mollie.

"Yeah," she said with a sigh, "don't mind me. It's just a bad morning, that's all. I hate rain—and I *detest* swim practice."

Mrs. Lewis glanced at her middle daughter in surprise. "Cindy Lewis, star freestyler and champion surfer, detests swim practice? Since when?"

"Yeah," Mollie chimed in, looking puzzled. "The last time I heard, you liked water better than anything—almost better than Grant even."

Cindy couldn't help grinning. "That was *before*," she replied, spooning up the last of her cereal.

"Before what?" her mother asked.

"Before Coach Sweeney came on the scene and started bugging me about priorities." Cindy got up from the table. "I'm driving to school this morning, shrimp," she said to Mollie, wanting to make up for her tacky remark about her sister's yellow outfit. "How about a ride?"

She'd expected Mollie to jump at the chance to ride to school instead of walking in the rain. But Mollie didn't answer right away, and when she did, she didn't show her usual enthusiasm for riding to school with Cindy.

"Well, I don't know," she said indecisively, looking out at the rain. "It's beginning to get a little lighter, don't you think? Maybe it'll slack off soon."

"But not before you get soaked to the skin," Cindy answered, a little surprised that Mollie hadn't bounced up and grabbed her books immediately, all set to go. Now that Cindy had her license, she often picked up Carey and Anna and Grant on her way to school, so the car was full and it didn't matter whether Mollie begged or not—she had to ride her bike.

But Mollie was still looking out at the rain. "I could wear my raincoat and boots and take a big umbrella ..." she said musingly.

"Or you could forget the boots and umbrella and ride in warm, dry comfort," Cindy coaxed, looking through her notebook to make sure she had her English homework. "Come on, don't be silly. The car's almost empty this morning. It's just Grant and me."

Mollie tilted her head thoughtfully. "Just Grant and you?"

"Right."

"Well, then, what would you say to another passenger?"

So *that* was why Mollie was holding back. She'd already made a date to walk with somebody else. Cindy sighed. "Sure, I guess so. Do we have to go out of our way to pick her up?"

Mollie blushed furiously. "No," she said, looking down. "He lives next door."

"Ah-ha!" Cindy hooted. "The truth comes out!"

"I'm just being helpful," Mollie said petulantly. "He comes from a very small school up in Oregon and he was worried about getting lost today. Vista High *is* pretty big, you know. And it can be awfully confusing on your first day. So I promised to show him where the office was and make sure that he got to his first class on time ..."

Mrs. Lewis looked up from clearing the table. "If you don't make up your mind about how you're getting to school, Mollie, there's a good chance that *you* won't be on time to *your* first class."

Panicked, Mollie looked at her watch and let out a screech. "Oh, my gosh," she cried, "it *is* late! I promised Chuck I'd pick him up five minutes ago!"

"Well, then, come on," Cindy said, and marched briskly to the door, with Mollie scurrying along behind and moaning about how horribly late it was.

Outside the principal's office, Mollie stood leaning against the wall and waiting for Chuck to pick up his course schedule. She had to admit that riding to school with Cindy and Grant had been a great idea. Chuck had hit it off with the others right away, and there'd been a lot of laughing and joking. It had been super when Sarah and Heather had seen her driving up with Cindy and Grant and Chuck—just as if all four of them were on a date. Of course, Sarah *had* expected Mollie to meet her by their lockers to go over their algebra problems, but Mollie knew her friend would understand how *urgent* it was to help another student on his first day at school. It was *so* important for a newcomer to feel oriented from the very beginning. She straightened up. Chuck was just coming out of the principal's office with his schedule in his hand. He definitely looked disoriented.

"First period advisory," he read aloud, "north wing, hallway D-1, room 214-B." He looked up. "It sounds like directions to the subway."

Mollie giggled, savoring the heady feeling of knowing something that the other person doesn't. "It's on the other side of the gym," she said importantly. "Come on, let's take a shortcut."

It was a minute after the first-period bell when Mollie slid into her seat next to Heather.

"So who *is* he?" Heather whispered curiously. "He's a real doll!"

"Yes, isn't he?" Mollie whispered back proudly. "He's new here—lives next door to me. I'm helping him find his way around."

"Lucky you," Heather said enviously. "I wish Baxter was that good-looking." Baxter Eblebaum was Heather's new boyfriend—well, not boyfriend exactly, since he hadn't asked her out yet. But Heather was hoping. She'd been hoping for the past three weeks, ever since he started calling her up. "Listen, speaking of Baxter," she added, "I really need some advice. How about lunch?"

But before Mollie could answer, the teacher

gave them a fierce look. "Is my hearing failing me," she said, "or did I hear the bell ring two minutes ago? Mollie and Heather, if you don't mind giving us your full attention, perhaps we can begin our lesson."

But Mollie's attention was elsewhere. All through class, she kept checking her watch, plotting how she was going to get Chuck to his next class and then get to hers—without being late. It was going to be tight, but she could do it.

And she did. She was waiting, breathless and feeling a little harried, outside Chuck's first-period class. And his second.

"You know," Chuck said as they sped through the halls between second and third periods, "you really don't have to do this, Mollie. I can ask somebody to point me in the right direction."

"Oh, that's okay, Chuck." Mollie panted, breathing through her nose to keep him from seeing how winded she was. "It's not out of my way." She made an extravagant gesture. "I've got all the time in the world."

At the end of third period, Sarah was waiting for her. After Mollie had apologized for not being around to talk over the algebra problems before school, Sarah said, "Listen, Heather wants us to have lunch with her today. She's having a terrible time with Baxter, and she wants to talk about it."

"Sure thing," Mollie said absently, checking her watch. "But I've got to bring Chuck along. I hope you don't mind."

"Chuck?" Sarah asked tensely. "Mollie Lewis, I just said that Heather wanted to talk about *Baxter*! How can she talk about him if you drag some strange guy to our table?"

"But I can't let Chuck eat by himself on his first day at school," Mollie pointed out reasonably. "And how would you like it if you had to go through the lunch line by yourself, trying to figure out whether something is edible or not?" She looked at her watch again. "Excuse me, Sarah, but I promised I'd help him find the cafeteria. See you there," she called over her shoulder as she skipped away. "Save us a table, will you?"

Halfway down the hall, she frowned. Sarah's last word had just registered. What was it? It had sounded really odd. Something like *"Arrgh!"*

The school cafeteria was already crowded when Cindy came in, looking for Grant and Duffy and the others. As she searched through the crowd, she spotted Mollie sitting with a couple of her girlfriends and Chuck. Mollie had both elbows on the table, talking animatedly to Chuck. Chuck himself squirmed a little uncomfortably under the barrage of Mollie's energetic and devoted attentions, while the two girls with them were talking to each other, turned pointedly away from their tablemates.

Cindy grinned sympathetically, wondering what was going through Chuck's mind. Maybe she should try to rescue him from Mollie, who appeared to be moving full steam ahead. And from the adoring look in Mollie's eyes, Cindy would bet her new surfboard that her baby sister was developing a queen-size crush on the boy next door.

But just at that moment Cindy caught sight of her friend Carey, sitting with a tall, red-haired boy at a table on the other side of the room. The red-haired boy, Duffy Duncan, saw her and stood up, using his hands like a megaphone.

"Hey, Lewis!" he bellowed. "Over here!"

Cindy gave up her thought of rescuing the object of Mollie's attentions and hurried to join her friends. Poor Chuck. She grinned to herself. He probably didn't realize it yet, but he had obviously become one of her sister's pet projects. And he seemed like such a *nice* guy, too.

"Listen, Mollie, it was *awfully* nice of you to introduce me to your friends at lunch," Chuck said as they walked hurriedly toward his fifth-period class. "And I really appreciate all your advice about what's fit to eat in the cafeteria. That's the kind of thing you don't want to learn by trial and error." He glanced at her sideways. "But I really had the feeling that I was monopolizing you. I'm sure the others wanted to talk with you, but they could hardly get a word in."

Mollie sniffed. Heather and Sarah *had* seemed a little put out for some reason or other, but she was sure they'd get over it. "It's no big deal," she said, "really. I know how awful it is to have to eat by yourself on the first day at a new school." It was true. Her first day at Vista High had been so hideous that she shuddered every time she thought about it. She didn't want Chuck to go through the same thing she'd gone through.

"Just the same," Chuck said insistently, "I don't think it's fair for me to take you away from your friends any longer. So from now on, why don't you just let me find my own way around? I mean, I'm really grateful, but sooner or later I'm going to have to manage by myself. I can't keep imposing on you forever." He grinned engagingly. "It's giving me this horrible guilty feeling."

"Nonsense!" Mollie said briskly. Wasn't it sweet of Chuck to worry so much about her feelings? She gave him her warmest smile. "What are friends for if not to help friends? Listen," she said hurriedly when they reached the door of his classroom, "the gang usually goes over to Pete's Pizzeria after school. If you'd like to meet some of the others—"

"Is Grant likely to be there?" Chuck asked with interest. "I really enjoyed talking to him this morning. I'd like to see him again."

Mollie hesitated. If Chuck and Grant got together, she'd probably get squeezed out of the conversation. But she had to tell the truth. "He might be," she said.

"Well, okay, I'll come then," Chuck said with a slight smile. He held up his hand to forestall Mollie's grin. "On one condition."

"Sure. What's that?"

"That you leave me to find things on my own for the rest of the afternoon."

"It's a deal," Mollie said. And then she added worriedly, "Are you sure you can find your next class?"

"Piece of cake," Chuck said confidently. "Meet you by the front door after school."

Mollie couldn't help it. "You *do* know where the front door is?"

Chuck made a wry face. "I hope so. If not, I'm in serious trouble."

"See you later." Mollie sighed happily, then floated away, her head in the clouds.

Chapter 5

"*Help!*" Cindy screeched at the pizzeria, throwing herself into the chair beside Carey. "I'm dying!"

Carey calmly looked up from her diet soda. "Oh, yeah? From what are you dying?"

"From Coach Sweeney, that's from what." Cindy sighed. "Can I have a sip?" Carey pushed the glass toward her, and Cindy stuck a straw into it and took a hard pull, emptying it. "She says the swim team *still* isn't high enough on my priorities. You know what she's telling me *now*?"

Carey laughed. "Let me guess. She says you have to give up sleeping at home and bring your sleeping bag to the pool so you can do laps at four A.M."

Cindy groaned. "Worse than that, much worse. It's totally rotten."

"What could be more totally rotten than laps at four A.M.?" Carey asked blankly.

Cindy rubbed her hand over her hair, still wet from her workout in the pool, and gave Carey an anguished look. "She says I should give up the water polo team."

Carey's mouth fell open. "The *polo* team?" she squeaked in disbelief. "But you *can't* give up the team! There won't be a polo team if you're not on it!"

Cindy shrugged. "Tell that to the coach," she said unhappily. "She says that I'm splitting myself into too many pieces, and my concentration is suffering. So I should give up water polo, since it's not a major sport but still takes time."

Carey looked indignant. "Hey, it's *my* major sport," she retorted tersely, red rising in her neck. "And the other guys on the team feel the same way. After all, we've worked pretty doggone hard to make water polo a sport that the rest of the kids will come out to watch." She slammed her fist on the table so hard that the empty glass fell over, spilling ice. "She can't do this, Cindy! We'll protest! We'll picket! Why, she isn't even the regular coach, she's just filling in! We'll demand—"

Feeling utterly miserable, Cindy held up her hand. "Not so fast. The trouble is that she didn't tell me I *had* to do it. She left it up to me."

"Up to you?"

"Yeah. Like, I'm supposed to decide."

"*You're* supposed to decide to give up the team?" Carey relaxed with a relieved smile. "Oh, well, why didn't you say so in the first place and save me from almost having a heart attack? It's easy then. All you have to do is tell her you've decided to stay on the team."

Cindy picked up the straw and began to weave it through her fingers, thinking about what had happened this afternoon at practice and feeling terribly mixed-up. "Yeah, well, maybe it isn't so easy, Carey. What if she's right? What if my swimming would improve if I did cut out some of the extra stuff I'm doing, like the polo team?" She sucked in her breath. "I mean, Liz Wright beat me twice last week, and tonight I just barely held my own against her." Her face flamed, remembering the smug look on Maureen's face when they climbed out of the pool.

"But you're better than Liz Wright," Carey said scornfully. She put a confident hand on Cindy's arm. "It's just a matter of getting your act together, that's all."

Cindy sighed. "I know. That's what the coach keeps telling me. Only now she says that getting my act together means giving up some of it."

"Just remember that we're your *friends,* not just your teammates," Carey reminded her firmly. "Think of all we've been through together. You can't give up the team, no matter what. We *need* you!"

Cindy said good-bye and stood up to leave. She knew that Carey was right. If she left the water polo team, they might as well kiss it good-bye. And if the team fell apart, how would Cindy feel? And Craig and Lou and Jean? They'd all be angry at her for letting them down.

"What a mess," she said to herself, pushing her way through the crowd. "What a horrible, *rotten* mess."

"What's a mess?"

Cindy turned around. It was Mollie, at a nearby table with Chuck and several others. They were all talking to one another, and Mollie looked a little left out. "It's too complicated to go into just now," Cindy said. "What's up?"

"We were just sort of hoping that you and Grant would stop in," Mollie said. She looked proudly at Chuck, who was deep in conversation with one of the guys, somebody Cindy recognized as being a member of the Ski Club. "I'm introducing Chuck around," she added earnestly. "You know, just to make sure that he meets all the right people and gets off to a good start."

"Uh-huh. Well, Grant won't be here today. He's working on his car. Want a ride home?"

Mollie shook her head. "No, thanks," she said. "I'll wait and walk with Chuck."

"Don't tell me," Cindy said with a skeptical laugh. "You just want to make sure he doesn't get lost. Right?"

"So what's wrong with giving him a few directions?" Mollie retorted, bristling.

"So maybe you should buy the guy a compass," Cindy quipped, and strode off.

Mollie made a face. She was used to Cindy's teasing, but sometimes it got a little old. She turned back to Chuck, who had stood up, still talking to the other guy, who was a junior and somebody she barely knew. "Are we getting ready to leave now?" she asked, getting up.

Chuck broke off his conversation. "Listen, Mollie, Roger and I are going over to his house to take a look at some ski stuff he's got for sale. See you later, huh?"

I think I should go along," Mollie said, suddenly feeling left out, "just to make sure that you—"

"I think," Chuck replied dryly, "that I can find my way home." He grinned and patted Mollie's shoulder. "But thanks for the offer, anyway. I appreciate it, Mollie."

Roger looked at Mollie with a glint of amusement in his eyes. "I'll take good care of him," he said. "I promise. He won't get lost."

Chuck reddened, and Mollie ducked her head, embarrassed. Why did everybody have to make such a big deal over the fact that she wanted to give a new friend a little help?

As she parked the car in the garage and went inside, Cindy couldn't help wishing that she'd open the kitchen door and find Nicole there, cooking something exotically French and humming cheerfully to herself. She *needed* her sister just now, needed to hear some of Nicole's levelheaded advice about what she should do about her dilemma.

But the kitchen was silent and empty except for an insistent Smokey, who came begging for a snack and wouldn't stop winding himself around Cindy's legs until she put some food in his dish. After she'd fed the cat, Winston bounded noisily in with his tongue lolling out and a practiced hungry-dog look on his face, and Cindy had to feed him, too. She was on her way upstairs when she saw two letters from Nicole lying on the hallway table. One was addressed to the family. The other was marked "Confidential to Cindy."

Delighted to find a letter of her own, Cindy ran upstairs and into her room, where she put a tape on her stereo and flopped down on the bed, grinning with anticipation. It was always such fun to read Nicole's letters because they were crammed with descriptions of all the exciting things she was doing—classes, people, parties—and peppered with her usual exuberant French. Since this one was marked "confidential," there must be something really important in it, Cindy thought. A new boyfriend, maybe? A juicy story about one of her roommates?

But whatever it was, the letter was exactly the antidote she needed to the bad mood she'd been in ever since she talked to Coach Sweeney. A letter from Nicole was almost as good as a phone call. It would certainly help to wash away the blues. Eagerly, Cindy ripped open the letter and started to read.

But her grin had faded by the end of the first sentence, for the letter didn't have any of Nicole's usual cheerfulness—in fact, it didn't sound at all like her.

To tell you the truth, things aren't as rosy here at Briarwood as I've pictured them in my other letters, ma chérie Cindy. In fact, I'm très worried about my schoolwork. I study all the time—even more than I did in high school, but it seems that all I receive in return is red ink, gallons of it, on every paper.

Cindy frowned. How could Nicole, always a superresponsible student, study *more* than she had in high school? There weren't that many more hours in the day, and she had to have some time for sleeping and eating and going to class, didn't she?

No matter how much I study, it doesn't seem to be enough. Midterms are coming up and I'm terribly worried that I might fail. And because I spend so much time studying, I never seem to get enough sleep. I'm tired all the time.

There were a couple of lines so heavily scratched out that Cindy couldn't read them, and then,

I don't know why I'm telling you all this, Cindy. I don't mean to worry you. But I am desperate for somebody to talk to, and my roommates don't seem to be having the same problems I'm having. Mon Dieu, *I wish you were here so we could talk. I'm so mixed up.*

It was signed simply, "*Adieu*, Nicole."

For a long while, Cindy stared at the letter, chewing her lip. Calm, cool Nicole, superstudent—worried about *failing* in college? Impossible! She gulped. Almost as impossible as Cindy Lewis, star freestyler, being warned by her coach that she had to give up water polo or risk losing her place on the swim team! What was happening to the superachieving Lewis girls? Was the law of averages finally catching up with them? Were they totally falling apart?

Downstairs, she heard the front door slam and then Mollie's footsteps, slow and dragging, on the stairs. The footsteps paused at Cindy's door, and the door slowly opened.

Cindy sat up and shoved Nicole's letter under her pillow. Although she had a sudden urge to share it with her sister and get her opinion, she wasn't sure she had a right to talk about Nicole's problems to anybody else.

So instead she asked teasingly, "Did you manage to get Chuck home safely?" and was immediately sorry when she saw the hurt expression on Mollie's face.

"No." Mollie sighed dolefully. "He went over to Roger's to look at some ski equipment." She sat down on the edge of the bed, her shoulders slumped, her expression dejected. "I guess he didn't want me to go along. He said he didn't need me."

"Well, he *does* have to make friends," Cindy pointed out, trying not to smile at her sister's obvious dejection. "I mean, I'm sure that you've been a big help to him, showing him around Santa Barbara, helping him get to his classes. But now he's got to meet people on his own."

"I know," Mollie agreed. "But I just wish he hadn't left me out when he and Roger went off, that's all."

"Yeah," Cindy said sympathetically. "Big crush, huh?"

"But that's not it at all," Mollie protested, pulling herself up straight. Then her shoulders drooped again, and she looked sideways at Cindy, her blue eyes growing large. "Do you think that's it?" she asked in a dramatic half whisper. "Do you really think I've got a crush on Chuck?"

"I think that's it," Cindy told her. "I saw that adoring look you were dishing out in the cafeteria at lunch." She reached for Mollie's hand and squeezed it. "It's better to admit it to yourself, shrimp, than to try to hide it. You don't want to make yourself look foolish, hanging around him like a moonstruck adolescent."

"But I thought I was just being helpful," Mollie said, looking confused. "How could I possibly mix up two such different things as being helpful and being in love? I mean, that's so *dumb*."

Cindy squeezed Mollie's hand again. "We all suffer from mixed emotions sometimes," she said with a little laugh, thinking about Nicole's letter and her own dilemma. "And to make it even worse, sometimes we don't even know how mixed-up we really are."

"Oh, Cindy." Mollie sighed, wrinkling her nose. "I feel so much better. It's so helpful to talk to you—almost as good as talking to Nicole."

"Thanks a lot, kid," Cindy said sarcastically. Then, with a giggle, she picked up her pillow and threw it at Mollie.

"Hey, isn't that a letter from Nicole?" Mollie asked, catching sight of the letter now lying in plain sight. "Oh, goodie!" she exclaimed. "Let me read it!"

"No!" Cindy exclaimed, snatching the letter and shoving it into the drawer of her bedside table. The thought of the letter sobered her and her giggles disappeared. "You've got your own letter downstairs. This one is confidential—to me."

Mollie pouted. "Confidential? I don't understand. Nicole doesn't write confidential letters."

"She did this time," Cindy insisted.

Mollie stood up. "Well," she said stiffly, "if you're going to be that way about it . . ." She went to the door and stood there for a minute, thinking. Then she grinned. "I guess I'll go call Chuck. I just got a terrific idea about what we could do tomorrow after school."

"Call Chuck?" Cindy asked, raising her eyebrow. "Hey, wait a minute. I thought you weren't going to chase him anymore."

"Whoever said a thing like that?" Mollie asked innocently. "I'm just glad to get un-confused about him, that's all." Her grin widened. "If it's a crush I've got, I might as well enjoy it, don't you think?" She started to go and then turned back again. "Listen, Cindy, I can't thank you enough for helping me to straighten this out in my mind."

Cindy groaned and buried her face in her hands.

Chapter 6

*E*arly the next morning, Mollie rang Chuck's doorbell. The sun was shining brightly, the birds were singing, and today was a new beginning—now that she understood her true feelings about Chuck. How could she have been so blind? Now that she thought about it, she could see that it had been love at first sight—at least as far as she was concerned. She'd felt all the symptoms, hadn't she? His good looks and his smile made her breathless, and she wanted to go out of her way to do nice things for him.

And while she couldn't be sure how Chuck felt about her, she just knew that things were going to work out. After all, they *were* neighbors. That meant they could see one another every day, ride their bikes to school together. Even if he wasn't sure how he felt about her right now, there was plenty of time for some chemistry to kick in.

Chuck's mother answered the door. "Good morning, Mollie," she said with a smile.

"Good morning." Mollie smiled brightly. "Is

Chuck ready? I thought maybe we could bike to school together this morning."

"Oh, I'm sorry," Mrs. Travis said regretfully, "but you've just missed him. Somebody named Roger came for him a few minutes ago."

"Oh." Suddenly a cloud seemed to slide across the sun and the birds stopped singing. "Oh well, I guess I'll see him at school then. Thanks." Mollie went down the sidewalk toward her bike, holding her head high until she heard Mrs. Travis close the door. Then she slumped in helpless dejection. It had happened again. He'd gone off without her. That must mean that he didn't like her. Mollie blinked the tears away. Their relationship was over—before it had even had a chance to begin!

But by the time she got to school, Mollie had begun to feel a little better. It was actually *good* that Chuck had gone off with Roger this morning, she'd decided. If he had some time for himself this morning, he might be more likely to accept her invitation for this afternoon.

"This afternoon?" Sarah asked when Mollie mentioned her plan. Sarah rolled her eyes. "What do you have in store for the guy this afternoon?"

Mollie closed her locker and leaned against it. "I thought this afternoon would be a good time to show him my favorite lookout point at the beach," she said with her eyes half-shut. She sighed dreamily, picturing the romantic sun setting into the restless blue water, the cooling breeze, Chuck's arm around her shoulder. . . .

"Oh-ho!" Sarah commented knowingly, tossing her reddish-brown hair. "The chase is on, is it?"

"It is not," Mollie retorted in an indignant tone, then fell into step beside Sarah as they walked down the hall toward their first-period advisory. "I'm just going to invite him to see what the beach looks like at sunset, that's all." And then she stopped, remembering what Cindy had said about being honest about her feelings. "Of course," she added truthfully, "if he's interested in a little romance, who am I to say no?"

"In my humble opinion," Sarah remarked, "what you ought to be saying is 'Whoa.' Look, I'm going to be blunt, Mollie. It is obvious that you've got a crush on this guy that won't quit, and that you're going to push him away if you chase after him. How about letting him come after *you* instead of you going after him?"

"But I'm *not* chasing him," Mollie said loftily. She ducked a paper airplane that came whizzing down the hall. "I am merely setting the stage for the future development of our relationship." She flipped her notebook open to the page where she had scrawled down Chuck's class schedule. "Let's see, I can probably catch him just before his second-period class."

"Well, don't say I didn't warn you," Sarah said. "And don't come crying to me about your broken heart." She turned and stalked away.

Before second period, Mollie was waiting in front of Chuck's classroom. He looked surprised when he saw her.

"Oh, hi, Mollie," he said. "How are you this morning?"

Mollie looked up at him, suppressing a sigh. No wonder she was in love with him—he was so handsome. "Oh, I'm fine," she said happily. "Wonderful, actually. Listen, Chuck, I was thinking. We really didn't have time on Saturday to take a look at the beach. I know this great place—a lookout point, sort of. How would you like to ride over there after school today?"

"Oh, I don't think ..." Chuck said, and then stopped, looking down at Mollie as she struggled to keep her disappointment from showing on her face. "Well," he said slowly, "if it means that much to you ... yeah, I guess I can make it, for a little while, anyway."

"Oh, Chuck, that's terrific!" Mollie exclaimed, suppressing the urge to put her hand on his arm. "I know you'll like this place—it's my very favorite spot. You can see for miles up and down the beach, and there are seagulls and pelicans and sometimes even dolphins out in the ocean." She knew she was babbling, but she couldn't help herself. She was so excited at the thought of the two of them going to the beach together to watch the sun set that she could hardly contain herself.

"Okay, Mollie," Chuck said. He backed up a little. "Listen, the Science Club is meeting today after school, so why don't I just meet you at your house? Okay if I pick you up at four-thirty?"

"That'll be perfect," Mollie said, and stood watching while he went into his classroom. Only when the bell rang, shattering her blissful reverie, did she realize that she was going to be late to her third-period class—again.

The afternoon sun was just as gloriously romantic as Mollie had remembered it, and as she and Chuck parked their bikes at the overlook and locked them, she shivered a little with anticipation. It was all working out exactly as she'd hoped. Here they were, together, alone, on the most romantic point along the entire Santa Barbara coastline just as the sun began its long descent toward the western horizon. To the north swept the soft, clean sands unbroken by rocks; to the south, jagged cliffs tumbled down to the sea, the waves breaking around them with a constant, muted roar. Along the shoreline, the gulls dipped and whirled, and an occasional pelican swept low along the waves, looking for a fishy snack.

"Hey, this is pretty neat!" Chuck said appreciatively. He wandered over to the edge and looked down. "Can we get down there? Down to that big rock, I mean? It looks like a perfect place to sit."

"Sure," Mollie said confidently. She started down the little path that led to the rocky ledge twenty feet below. Once there, they sat down, side by side, and leaned against the sun-warmed rock. Mollie closed her eyes and tried to calm the nervous flutter in her stomach. It was such a beautiful spot: private, secluded, *romantic*. Did Chuck feel the tug of romance as strongly as she did? Would he hold her hand? Would he ... would he kiss her? Mollie's heart executed a triple somersault at the dizzying thought of his arm around her shoulders, his lips coming closer to hers—

Chuck nudged her sharply with his elbow. "Hey, Mollie, what's that?"

Mollie sat up and opened her eyes. Chuck was peering through a pair of binoculars at something far out at sea.

"What's what?"

He handed her the binoculars and pointed. "See? Out there? It looks like a tower or something."

"Oh, that," Mollie said. "That's just an oil rig. There are lots of them around here."

"Oh," Chuck said. He put the binoculars back to his eyes and began to scan the horizon again, as Mollie leaned against the warm rock and closed her eyes, giving herself once again to her imagination. Chuck's arm around her shoulders, his lips coming closer to hers, his voice soft and gentle and caressing—

"Hey, wow!" Chuck shouted excitedly. "There's a *whale* out there! I just saw it spout!"

Mollie opened her eyes again. "Yeah," she said, "they hang around here sometimes. People go out on charter boats to look at them."

Chuck stood up and pulled a field guide out of his pocket. "Listen, I'm going to walk down to the beach and see if I can identify some seashells and stuff," he said. "But you look so comfortable dozing there in the sun that I don't want to disturb you. Stay where you are—and if I'm not back in about ten minutes, go on home without me. I'll find my own way back."

And with a pat on her shoulder and a quick grin, he was gone.

For a minute, Mollie looked after him, her mouth dropping open. And then she shut her mouth, her lips drawing together in a tight line. So much for a soft, lovely sunset. So much for romance. A half hour later, she stood up. She was bored with watching the whales spout, her rear end ached from sitting on the hard rocks, and it was obvious that Chuck wasn't coming back before dark. She climbed the path, unlocked her bike, and rode home. There was a giant, aching lump in her throat and it hurt to swallow.

When Cindy got home from her workout in the pool she was glad to see that her mother was already in the kitchen fixing supper.

"How was school today?" Mrs. Lewis asked, turning away from the refrigerator with an armload of salad fixings.

Cindy made a face. "Yuck," she said. "Double yuck." She sighed. Since a heart-to-heart with Nicole was out, a good, old-fashioned mother-daughter talk might help. "Listen, Mom, I've got this terrible problem. Coach Sweeney says I should give up the water polo team in order to concentrate on my swimming."

Mrs. Lewis raised her eyebrows. "Give up water polo? Isn't that kind of drastic? Sounds like a hard choice to me."

"Oh, boy, is it ever." Cindy sighed. "If I quit water polo, the kids on the team will kill me. If I don't quit, Coach Sweeney will kill me." She gave her mother a tentative look. "I don't suppose you have any advice," she asked hopefully.

Mrs. Lewis shook her head. "I wish I did. That's a terrible dilemma, Cindy. It's one of those choices that—"

At that moment the back door opened and Mollie came in. "Hi," she said gloomily, dropping her sweater on a chair.

Mrs. Lewis looked from one daughter to the other. "I'd say that the Lewis girls *both* had a hard day." She laughed sympathetically. "Maybe I'd better make that apple pie I was thinking about. Would that cheer anybody up?"

Mollie managed a weak smile. "Maybe," she said. She sat down across from Cindy. "But I doubt it."

Mrs. Lewis came over and put a hand on Mollie's forehead. "Are you coming down with something?" she asked. "Fever? Sore throat?"

Cindy looked at her sister. "Let me guess," she said. "It's Chuck, isn't it?"

"He turns out to be more interested in seashells and whales than he is in me," she said.

"Well," Cindy suggested, "maybe he's just not ready for a relationship just now. After all, he just moved here and he probably doesn't feel like getting involved with somebody right away. If you stop bugging him and give him time to get settled, maybe he'll feel different in a week or two."

Mollie brightened a little, some of her natural optimism returning. "Do you really think that'll happen?" she asked.

Cindy shrugged. "Who knows? But it's worth a try, isn't it?" She sighed, wishing that she could come up with a resolution to her problem that sounded half as good as the one she'd just offered to Mollie.

Just then the phone rang and Mrs. Lewis reached for it. "Hello," she said, and then, "Yes, this is Nicole's mother." And then she paused for a moment, listening. As she did so, she began to look worried.

From the table, Cindy watched her mother with increasing concern, suddenly remembering the letter in her bureau drawer upstairs. Nicole had sounded so down, so uncharacteristically gloomy. Had something happened to her? What was going on?

"I see," Mrs. Lewis said. She cleared her throat. "What does the doctor say?"

The doctor? Cindy's heart seemed to stop beating, and on the other side of the table, Mollie's eyes were huge and her face was white. Was something wrong with Nicole? Why did she need a doctor?

"I see," Mrs. Lewis said. "Yes, tomorrow will be fine." She jotted something down on the notepad beside the phone and then said, "Please tell Nicole to rest and not to worry. We'll be at the airport to meet her." She hung up the phone and turned to them, her eyes dark with worry.

"Mom, what's wrong?" Cindy asked. She'd never before seen such an expression on her mother's face.

"Is Nicole sick or something?" Mollie cried. "Is she coming home?"

"Yes, Nicole's sick," Mrs. Lewis said raggedly. "She's got a case of mononucleosis."

"Monowhatsis?" Mollie wailed. "It sounds *horrible*! Can she ... can she *die* from it?"

"Mono!" Cindy exclaimed. "Is it serious?"

Mrs. Lewis collected herself. "Mononucleosis is when your glands get swollen and you get a fever and you're tired all the time," she told Mollie. "But you don't die from it." She turned to Cindy. "The doctor at the Briarwood infirmary doesn't think it's a serious case. She's got to get more rest, though, than she can get at the dorm. So she's coming home for a couple of weeks."

Cindy stared at her mother. Nicole was sick. How awful! But she was coming home! Suddenly Cindy felt an enormous sense of relief, as if a giant stone about the size of their house had just rolled off her shoulders. Nicole always knew how to solve problems, even the thorniest ones. Nicole could help her decide what to do!

Chapter 7

It only took about thirty seconds for Cindy to begin feeling terribly guilty about the way she'd reacted. Nicole was sick and needed rest—*that* was why she was coming home. Cindy made up her mind that she wasn't going to say a word about her problems. The important thing—the *only* thing—was for Nicole to get well again, just as quickly as possible.

That's what Carey said, too, when Cindy told her at lunch that Nicole was coming home.

"Oh, my gosh," she exclaimed. She swallowed a bite of yogurt and stared at Cindy. "Listen, Cindy, if she stays out for two whole weeks, she might have to drop out for the entire semester! That's what happened to my cousin Andrea—she got sick and had to come home and she fell so far behind that she *couldn't* go back."

Cindy began to chew on her lip. She hadn't thought about it that way. What if Nicole had to drop out of school?

"Listen, Cindy," Carey said, leaning forward urgently, "I told some of the kids on the water polo team about what Coach Sweeney told you. And they were really upset. They wanted me to let you know that they think you should just tell her to stuff it. We need you on the team—we can't do without you!"

Cindy sighed. "I know," she said unhappily, picking at her salad. "I don't want to let the team down. But I need a few more days to think it over, so will you stop bugging me about it?"

"Okay," Carey said reluctantly, "as long as you remember how much the team is counting on you." She went back to her yogurt. "When's Nicole arriving?"

Cindy glanced at her watch. "Just about now," she said. "The folks are going to take Nicole to see our family doctor straight from the airport. She'll be home by the time I get back from swim practice."

When Cindy got home that afternoon, she slipped quietly into the kitchen and shut the door carefully behind her. Her mother and father were sitting at the kitchen table drinking tea, their expressions serious.

"Did she get here?" Cindy whispered worriedly. "How is she?"

"No need to whisper," Mr. Lewis said. He pushed his glasses up on his forehead and leaned back. "Yes, she got here just fine. And she seems pretty much okay, if you ask me. A little thin, maybe, but that's to be expected." He smiled at his wife. "After all, the Briarwood cafeteria can't be anything like her mother's cooking. But I've got to say that she certainly looks *pretty*. You'd hardly know she was sick."

"We took her to Dr. MacIntyre right away, of course," Mrs. Lewis said. "He gave her some more antibiotics and said that she's not contagious and should be as good as new in a few days, if she gets plenty of rest."

"Thank heaven!" Cindy exclaimed with a sigh of relief. "Is she upstairs?"

"Yes," Mrs. Lewis said, then she got up to pour another cup of tea. "I think she's asleep. But you might look in on her all the same. She seems a little depressed over all the work she's missing. So see if you can cheer her up, huh?"

"I'll try," Cindy promised. She looked at her mother. "Uh, Mom, is there any chance that Nicole won't be able to make up her work? Carey's cousin Andrea got sick and had to drop out. That's not going to happen to Nicole, is it?"

Mrs. Lewis shook her head emphatically. "I phoned her dean this morning. Nicole's apparently been having some difficulty with her courses, but if she takes advantage of these two weeks to review her classwork, she ought to be able to pick it up again without any problem."

"That's good," Cindy said. "It would be awful if she had to drop out of Briarwood now, after she looked forward to it so much."

She left the kitchen and tiptoed hurriedly up the carpeted stairs, trying not to make any noise. The door to Nicole's room was open a crack and Cindy pushed it wider, stepping in. Nicole was lying in bed, wearing her favorite old pink flannel pajamas. Her long, chestnut-colored hair fell like a veil over her face. Her eyes were shut and her dark lashes were smudges against her pale cheeks. Cindy sucked in her breath. Her sister *was* thin, and there were lines of weariness around her mouth, but she looked prettier than Cindy had ever seen her before. Not wanting to wake her, Cindy turned to leave.

But at that moment the door squeaked, and Nicole's eyes flew open.

"Cindy!" she exclaimed, sitting up straight in bed. *"Mon Dieu!* I'm so glad to see you!"

With a delighted cry, Cindy flung herself at her sister. "Oh, I'm so happy that you're home!" she cried, enveloping her in a huge hug. And then quickly, "I mean, I'm sorry you're sick and you have to come home, but ..."

"I know." Nicole sighed and pulled the pillows behind her so that she could sit up against them. "I wouldn't have left school if the doctor hadn't positively insisted. But I'm glad to be home, too." She opened her arms expansively, as if to gather everything in. "My room feels so wonderful—it's like being in heaven."

Cindy looked around. She understood why Nicole said that. Her room was so much like her, with its stylishly tasteful decor, its neat, graceful femininity. The wall over the desk was papered with photos and maps of France, which Nicole always called her "spiritual home;" the bed was covered with a thick, lavender Laura Ashley spread and crocheted pillows; and there was a soft white rug on the floor. The room even *smelled* like Nicole, with the soft, delicate scent of blooming violets in the air.

"Well, it's *wonderful* to have you here," Cindy said, giving her sister another hug. She laughed a little, despite the lump in her throat and sat back on the edge of the bed. "I guess I hadn't realized how much I actually missed you until you came back."

"Tell me about—" Nicole began.

"I want to hear all about—" Cindy said at the same time.

The girls stopped and then laughed.

"You first," Cindy said. "I want to know all about college, what your roommates are really like, whether the boys are as good-looking as you claimed they were in your letters—the whole, entire, unvarnished *truth,* from beginning to end."

Nicole's smile faded and she leaned back wearily against the pillows. "Do you remember last summer," she asked, "when I went to Montreal for that special honors course?"

Cindy giggled. "Oh, boy, do I!" she declared. She rubbed her backside ruefully. "I can still feel all those bruises." Cindy and Mollie had gone along with Nicole, and Cindy had found a Canadian ice-hockey team to work out with. Even though she'd quickly discovered that the hard ice wasn't as forgiving as water, she'd kept at it— bumps, bruises, and all.

"Yes, well, I took plenty of bruises, too, if you'll recall," Nicole said with a sigh. "I thought I was pretty super, graduating at the top of my high school class, collecting all those A's in French. But when I got to Montreal and came up against some real competition, I realized that I had a lot more to learn." She paused for a moment, reflecting. "Well, if Montreal was hard, Briarwood is *très impossible*."

"But that's just what I don't understand," Cindy said. "You know more French than anybody, and your other grades were super, too. You ought to be a standout at Briarwood."

"But at Briarwood everybody's high school grades were super, and all the students in my French class are *très bon*." Nicole made a face. "And it's not only the difficulty and the competition, but the distractions, too. My roommates love to party, the student union schedules a movie every night—and often wonderful French cinema—and there are concerts and art exhibits and dances and—"

"I see what you mean," Cindy said when Nicole paused for breath. "It sounds wonderful."

"It *is* wonderful—at least it was until midterm. Then, when you realize that you're light-years behind in your homework, and exams are looming over you like a black cloud, and you've blown a whole semester's food allowance on a new French book—well, maybe it doesn't seem quite so wonderful anymore. And I've been lonesome, too, for my family and all the good friends I left behind." She pounded her fist on the spread. "And now I've got to be out for a whole two weeks, and I'll *never* get caught up!"

Nicole lay back against the pillows, looking exhausted and dejected, and Cindy suddenly felt guilty. She'd promised her mother to talk about cheerful things, and instead she'd let Nicole talk on and on, wearing herself out and thinking discouraging thoughts about all the work she was missing.

"Oh, I'm sure you'll catch up," she said lightly. "Now that you're here, all you have to do is hide out in your room, let us wait on you hand and foot, do a little homework when you feel like it, and sleep the rest of the time. What a break!" she added enviously, thinking of her own troubles. "I wish I could take a vacation for a couple of weeks."

Nicole smiled a little and patted her sister's cheek. "So what's up in your life these days, *ma chérie*? How is Grant?"

"Oh, Grant's just fine," Cindy said, looking away.

"And school? And Mollie?"

"School's okay, and Mollie's okay, too, even though she's got a colossal crush on the new guy next door." She laughed a little. "I'm sure that Mollie will survive, but I don't know about the guy. He's really in for it."

Nicole gave her an insistent look. "Well, then, what is it?"

Cindy stared at her sister. "What do you mean, what is it?"

"So what's bothering you?"

Cindy took a deep breath. Did her sister have radar or something? "What makes you think that something's bothering me?" she asked as lightly as she could. "As a matter of fact, everything's super. Couldn't be better."

Nicole shook her head, frowning a little. "Listen, Cindy, I haven't lived with you for almost seventeen years without knowing when you've got something on your mind. Now, come on, come clean."

"I wasn't going to tell you," Cindy said defensively. She pulled her knees up to her chin and hugged them. "I didn't want to worry you." She looked at Nicole sideways, trying to decide whether she should tell her.

"Don't worry about worrying me."

Cindy heaved a gigantic sigh. "Well, things haven't been so great at the pool for the last couple of weeks. Coach Lawford is out indefinitely—he's had back surgery—and this other coach, a woman named Sweeney, has taken over. She's real tough, and she's got it into her head that there are too many distractions in my life. She says I have to concentrate more of my attention on my swimming."

Nicole hooted. "This is news? Cindy, *ma chérie*, your life is one long maze of distractions." She began to tick items off on her fingers. "There's Grant, of course, and then there's surfing, wind surfing, sailing, skiing, softball, not to mention ice hockey, and—"

"You can spare us the list." Cindy sighed. "I know I overdo it sometimes. But Coach Sweeney says I have to give something up, and she's decided it should be water polo."

Nicole frowned. "But what would happen to the team if you quit? I seem to remember that you sort of hold things together for them." Then she said softly, "Oh, yes, I see. *That's* your problem."

"Yeah," Cindy said unhappily. "It's a real dilemma, isn't it?" She turned to Nicole. "What should I do?" she burst out. "Carey is really upset with me. She says that if I leave the team, I'll be forsaking all my friends. But if I don't, Coach

Sweeney may drop me from the swimming team!" There were tears in the corners of her eyes and she rubbed them away with the backs of her hands. "I really need your advice."

Nicole looked sympathetic. "Well, for starters, I guess I'd tell you not to let Carey make you feel responsible for what happens to the water polo team. If they're true competitors, they'll pull themselves together and become even stronger after you're gone. If they're not, and if they fall apart the minute you leave, then they weren't much of a team in the first place."

"Yeah, I see what you mean," Cindy said thoughtfully, propping her chin on her knees. "So you're saying that I should just step back and let them sink or swim—so to speak."

Nicole gave her a steady look. "No, not really," she said. "I'm just suggesting that, whatever you do, don't do it just because you feel *guilty*. This decision is too important to be made out of a sense of guilt. Maybe you should leave the water polo team and concentrate on your swimming. But if you do, you should do it because you feel a responsibility to yourself to be the best swimmer you can be, and not afraid of what will happen to the team."

Cindy let go of her knees and leaned back on her hands. "Oh, now I see what you're saying. You're telling me that I should give up all my friends in water polo and focus my attention on swimming."

Nicole was staring out the window. "No, not that, either," she said softly, almost as if she was talking to herself. "I said the team will make it without you—but will you make it without the team? Without your *friends*, I mean."

Cindy stared at her sister, shaking her head in frustration. "Look, Nicole, maybe I'm confused, but I thought I just heard you say that if I had to give up my friends to be the best, I should do that, too."

Nicole reached for Cindy's hands, her eyes intent on her sister's face. "There you are," she said. "You've said it more clearly than I could. Do you want to be the best swimmer *even if* it means giving up your friends?"

The light dawned. "So it's not a matter of the water polo team at all, is it?" Cindy said, half to herself. "It's a choice between narrowing everything down to swimming or to having friends, isn't it?"

A smile washed across Nicole's face. "Congratulations," she said. "*Now* you can see what the real question is." A shadow crossed her face and she stopped to think for a moment. "And perhaps," she added, again as if she was talking to herself, "you may decide that it's better to have real friends in your life than to be a superstar on the swim team."

Chapter 8

"*N*icole! Nicole! Are you awake?" Nicole recognized Mollie's familiar squeal as her sister pounded eagerly up the stairs and into Nicole's bedroom.

"If I wasn't awake already, I am now," Nicole said, laughing, as Mollie launched herself at the bed.

"Oh, Nicole," Mollie exclaimed, "I've missed you so much!" She stared at her sister, her eyes getting wide. "You look so pretty! Nicole, you're beautiful!"

"*Merci, ma petite!*" Nicole replied, touched by her sister's admiration. She held Mollie off at arm's length, gazing at her. "But maybe not so *petite* after all."

"But I've been so *careful* with my diet!" Mollie cried. "I haven't had even a potato chip in weeks, and—"

Nicole laughed and gave her sister an extra squeeze. "Not that kind of growing, silly! You're getting taller; you're stretching out. And you're prettier, too." She turned to Cindy with a grin. "I'll bet Mollie has boyfriends coming out her ears."

Mollie stuck out her tongue at Nicole. "I wish," she muttered, pulling her feet up and sitting cross-legged on the foot of Nicole's bed. "Actually, I'd settle for just one."

"Oh!" Nicole exclaimed, leaning back and letting Cindy adjust her pillows. "Is this special interest the guy next door that Cindy was telling me about?"

"Yes," Mollie said excitedly. "His name is Chuck and—" Then she stopped for a second, and when she spoke again, her voice had changed. "Except that he's not really a boyfriend," she added sadly. She turned to Cindy, obviously wanting to change the subject. "Cindy, did you tell Nicole about—"

Cindy held up her hand. "Hey, wait a minute, shrimp. What do you mean, he's not a boyfriend? Didn't I see the two of you eating lunch together today? You looked pretty cozy to me."

Mollie squirmed under Cindy's curious look. "We weren't really eating lunch together," she said. "He just stopped at the table for a minute to say hello, that's all."

It was true—that was what had happened. Of course, Mollie had been delighted when he sat down to talk, and she'd taken his gesture as an apology for his rudeness the evening before, when he'd abandoned her at the beach. After a night and a morning of bleak, utter dejection, she had spent the afternoon feeling hopeful again—well, a little, anyway.

But she wasn't ready to tell Cindy and Nicole

all of this. They would laugh and tease her and want to know how she felt about Chuck. And for some reason, she just didn't feel like sharing her feelings about him. Cindy and Nicole had never had any trouble attracting boys; they couldn't know how it felt to like somebody and not be sure whether that person liked you back.

But Nicole couldn't know what was going through Mollie's mind. "Come on, Mollie, give," she urged with a smile, curious about her sister's reluctance to talk about Chuck. Usually Mollie bubbled on and on about what was going on in her life and you practically had to put a gag in her mouth to get her to stop. "Don't hold back. At least tell me what he's like. Is he good-looking? What does he do for fun?"

"Oh, I guess he's good-looking enough," Mollie said evasively.

"You guess?" Cindy chortled. "Listen, Nicole," she said in a teasing voice, obviously baiting Mollie, "wait until you cast your eyes on this guy—he's real movie-star stuff. Tall, with humongous shoulders"—she held out her hands to demonstrate—"and sandy hair and green eyes and—"

"Hey," Mollie said, "don't you think you're overdoing it a little?"

"Grant had better watch out." Nicole laughed. "It sounds like *two* of the Lewises have crushes on Prince Charming. I can't wait to meet him—when I'm well enough to handle his devastating charm."

Mollie looked at Nicole as she and Cindy began to talk about the things that were going on at

Vista High. Something new had occurred to her—
something new and unsettling. Now that she
thought about it, she wasn't at all sure that she
wanted her sister to meet Chuck. Nicole was beautiful, more beautiful than she'd been when she
went away to college, and far more beautiful than
Mollie, who often felt like a fluffy little puppy dog
alongside her glamorous sister. She could handle
Cindy because Cindy was clearly occupied with
Grant and didn't have time in her life for other
boys. But since Nicole had broken up with her
boyfriend Mark last year, she hadn't had *any*
boyfriends—and Chuck certainly *was* good-looking,
good-looking enough for Nicole, even. While Mollie was a generous person, she didn't think she
was generous enough to want to share Chuck
with anybody, especially her sister Nicole.

Mollie shook herself. What nonsense she was
thinking! Even if she was interested in Chuck, he
wasn't her boyfriend, so she didn't have any right
at all to feel possessive about him. And, anyway,
Nicole was going to be shut up in her bedroom,
resting, for the next couple of weeks, and after
that she'd be headed back to Briarwood. So what
was the problem?

Still, Mollie's face remained thoughtful, and Nicole noticed that her sister was uncharacteristically quiet for the next few minutes.

Nicole's and Cindy's conversation was interrupted by a tap on the door. It was Mrs. Lewis,
holding a big basket.

"Dad had to go back to the office this evening
to catch up on the work he missed this after-

noon," she said. "So I thought we'd have an old-fashioned indoor picnic right here in Nicole's room. Sandwiches, potato salad, deviled eggs—the works. What do you say?"

Mollie perked up immediately. "An indoor picnic." She giggled, clapping her hands. "Just like when we were kids!"

Nicole laughed, too. "Do you remember our rainy-day picnics?" she asked her mother. "When we used to dress up our dolls and get you to make a picnic for us up in the attic, with little sandwiches and fruits and cookies?" She sighed nostalgically. "Those were *wonderful* days. Everything seemed so simple back then, when all we had to do was *pretend* we were grown-ups."

Cindy wrinkled her forehead. "It *was* simple back then," she replied emphatically. "All we had to worry about was keeping our dolls separate and not getting into too much trouble. We didn't have to think about making choices."

"And we didn't have to think about boyfriends," Mollie agreed mournfully.

"Have you forgotten the little Peterson boy down the block?" Mrs. Lewis asked with a chuckle, spreading a white cloth on the foot of Nicole's bed. "Don't you remember, Mollie, that you and Cindy *both* liked him and that you got into a fight one day over who was going to go to the park with him?"

"We didn't," Cindy said indignantly, hands on her hips.

"You did, too," Nicole said, giggling. "I remember breaking the two of you up. You had a fistful of Mollie's hair and you were yanking it so hard I thought you were going to pull it out."

"I remember Cindy pulling my hair," Mollie said reminiscently, "and Nicole coming along and being bossy and making her stop. But I didn't remember why we were fighting." She looked at Nicole. "Was it actually over a *boy*?"

"It was actually over a boy," Nicole assured her. "He was cute, too, as I remember. He had big brown eyes and curly brown hair and big scabs on his knees. He loved to roller-skate," she added in explanation. "That's why Cindy hung around with him."

Mollie shook her head mournfully. "And I don't even remember his name."

"It's just as well forgotten." Mrs. Lewis laughed, pouring glasses of milk. "You're all too grown-up for kids' stuff like that."

Cindy sighed. "Right. Now we've got adult stuff to worry about." She reached for a cheese sandwich from the platter that Mrs. Lewis had put on the bed. "Like whether to stay with the swim team or the water polo team."

And whether Chuck likes me or not, Mollie thought, helping herself to some of her mother's famous potato salad.

"And whether I'll manage to pass my exams at Briarwood," Nicole said somberly. She looked around at her family, feeling their warmth pulling her in, making her feel loved and wanted in a way that she hadn't felt for months. She sighed. "Listen, everybody, being home with all of you is absolutely *magnifique*! Really, it's enough to make me want to stay here and not go back at all."

"I keep telling you, you don't have anything to worry about," Cindy said brusquely. "When you get back you'll pass your exams with flying colors." Then a new thought seemed to occur to her, and she added inquiringly, "Unless you don't really *want* to go back?"

Nicole glanced at her mother. Did she want to go back to Briarwood? It was a question that had lingered at the back of her mind ever since the doctor had ordered her home. Guiltily, feeling angry at herself for even entertaining the idea of being a quitter, she tried to push the thought away, but she couldn't. Did she want to go back to Briarwood, where her professors seemed to have utterly *zilch* sympathy for her struggles to achieve and her roommates were usually too busy with their own problems to care about hers? Or did she want to stay here, with her sisters and her parents? If she stayed, she could always go to UCLA, where Mark and her other friends had gone. If she stayed—

Mollie's disbelieving voice cut into her thoughts. "You're actually thinking of staying home? After all the months you planned to go to Briarwood, and all the effort it took to get in?" Mollie shook her head. "I just don't believe—"

"Hey, come on, Mollie," Cindy interrupted, "give Nicole a break. After all, she's tired and she's been under the weather. You don't like having to make big decisions when you're not feeling up to par, do you?"

"That's right," Mrs. Lewis said firmly. She handed around a plate of deviled eggs. "Nicole doesn't have to decide *anything* right now. She's on vacation from all decision-making."

Nicole gave her mother a grateful smile. That's what she needed right now—a vacation from making decisions. Unfortunately, though, that's all it would be: a vacation. Sooner or later, the decision would have to be faced. And what would she do then?

Chapter 9

"I can see," Sarah said, marking the place in her book with her finger, "that you *definitely* have a problem." She leaned across the library table toward Mollie, pursing her lips accusingly. "Didn't I warn you that this thing would develop into a problem?"

Mollie sighed. "Yes, you warned me," she replied. "I just don't agree that it's a problem, that's all."

"But do you ever listen?" Sarah continued, not paying any attention to Mollie's reply. "No, of course not," she said, answering her own question. "You never listen. You're always moving full speed ahead without thinking about where you might wind up. And now here you are, with a terminal case of the Big Crush, asking me for advice again!"

"Listen, Sarah," Mollie hissed, looking around to make sure that Mrs. Phelps, the librarian, wasn't listening, "I'm not asking for the lecture of the century. I just asked a very simple question: What do you think about my asking Chuck to the turnabout dance next week?"

The turnabout dance, to which the girls asked the guys, was always a big event at Vista. The year before, Mollie had felt too uncertain about guys to even consider asking one to the dance. She still felt uncertain, and that's why she had asked Sarah's advice—although she was beginning to wish she hadn't.

"Well, here's what I think," Sarah answered, "and it's the same thing I thought the last time you asked me. I think that you're making an idiot of yourself chasing after Chuck and that he is embarrassed because you pay so much attention to him. And as long as he's embarrassed, he's going to keep on running just as hard and as fast as his legs will take him—in the opposite direction."

Mrs. Phelps frowned primly and shook her head at them. Sarah suddenly assumed a studious look and hunched over her book.

Mollie propped her chin on her hands and fixed her eyes on her book, but she wasn't reading. She *had* followed Sarah's advice, and Cindy's advice, too—at least for a day or two. She hadn't spoken to Chuck since he'd stopped at their lunch table to say hello, two whole days ago. She'd *watched* him, yes, from a distance, like yesterday afternoon when she'd sat out on the front porch while he mowed the lawn next door.

But for a whole forty-eight hours she had resisted the temptation to call him on the phone, hoping he would call her. For Mollie, forty-eight hours without talking to Chuck seemed like an eternity, and the week ahead, without the prospect of a single word with him, stretched out like a dry, empty desert with no oasis in sight. It was awful. She sighed. Cindy was right. It had to be love.

The librarian went back to her desk and Mollie leaned toward Sarah. "Listen, so what if it is a crush?" she whispered. "Is there a law against liking somebody? And why shouldn't I ask him to the dance? It's the friendly thing to do, isn't it? Wouldn't you hate to be a guy in a brand-new school where you didn't know a single, solitary girl and have to worry about whether anybody's going to ask you to the dance?"

Sarah looked up from her book. "No, there's no law against liking somebody," she countered with a little more sympathy. "But it's stupid to mess up your chances with somebody by chasing him. And if you want my honest opinion," she added, "I'd say that Chuck Travis isn't the kind of guy who stays awake nights worrying about whether he's going to be asked to some silly dance. Anyway, I'll bet he knows plenty of girls by now. In fact," she said casually, "I saw him walking down the hall with Sharon Woodruff this morning."

Mollie's heart sank down to the toes of her pink sneakers. Sharon Woodruff was the captain of the pep squad, very nice and very cute. "You mean, you think Sharon might ask Chuck to the dance?" she asked, alarmed. She looked up at the clock. It was almost time for the bell to ring. "Maybe I'd better go find him right after this period and ask him *now* before she does!" With a groan, she ran her fingers through her hair, adding desperately, "If it isn't too late already!"

Sarah closed her book with a disgusted *thump*. "I tell you, Mollie, you've gone totally berserk. You're going to mess up this thing for good if you don't let it develop naturally."

But Mollie wasn't listening to Sarah's warning. She was leafing frantically through her notebook for Chuck's class schedule. Where was his next class?

Cindy picked up her bookbag and slung it over her shoulder as she headed from history class to the gym for P.E. It was Friday, which meant badminton, and she usually looked forward to it. But today she was depressed. Even though Nicole had given her a new slant on her problem, Cindy wasn't a smidgen closer to figuring out what to do. In fact, every time she thought about it, things seemed to get more and more snarled, like a tangle of spaghetti. Swimming, Coach Sweeney, Carey, the water polo team—they were all jumbled together in her mind.

Behind her, Carey called, "Hey, Cindy, wait up!"

Cindy slowed reluctantly. Carey was the last person on earth she wanted to see just now. But it wouldn't help to let her friend know that. So with a great effort, she plastered a smile on her face and turned around. "Hi," she said with artificial cheerfulness. "How's it going?" The question came out sounding ragged.

"Okay," Carey said, falling into step with Cindy. "On your way to P.E.?" Her voice sounded as frayed as Cindy felt.

"Uh-huh," Cindy replied. "Today's badminton, you know."

Carey sighed. "I know," she said. "I wish I were as good in it as you are."

An awkward, uncomfortable silence hung in the air between them. Cindy began to walk faster.

"Uh, listen, Cindy," Carey said, hurrying to catch up, "I don't want to bug you, but do you think we could talk about the water polo team?"

Cindy's feelings of frustration suddenly overwhelmed her and she whirled on Carey, her temper flaring. "Will you cool it about the team?" she snapped. "Just leave me alone, will you?"

Carey took a step backward, her eyes widening. "Hey," she said, "there's no need to get so upset. I just wanted to tell you that—"

"I don't *care* what you wanted to tell me," Cindy interrupted, her hands on her hips, her eyes flashing. "I don't want to talk about it, and that's that!"

"Well, if you feel that way about it," Carey said huffily, "I guess maybe you'd better walk to class by yourself."

"That's how I feel," Cindy replied, stalking away and leaving Carey standing in the middle of the hall staring after her. But the anger that had flashed so suddenly was already beginning to seep away, leaving her feeling sorry for what she had said. Why couldn't she control her temper?

At that moment, she rounded the corner and crashed into Mollie, who had her head down and was walking very slowly as if she were in a dream. Mollie and her books went flying and landed with a loud *oomph* in the middle of the hallway.

"Mollie!" Cindy exclaimed, startled, as Mollie

began to pick herself up. "You're such a bubble-head. Why weren't you looking?"

Mollie sniffled. "Because," she said, gathering up her books.

Cindy peered at her. "Are you crying?" she asked, bending over to help. "What's wrong? Are you hurt?"

"I'm not crying," Mollie said. She pulled out a tissue and wiped her nose. "I've got a cold, that's all." She sniffled again. "Or maybe it's an allergy." She gave an artificial-sounding sneeze.

"You *are* crying," Cindy insisted, seeing the tears in Mollie's eyes. "Did something happen?" She looked up just in time to see Chuck coming toward them, walking with Sharon Woodruff. Sharon was saying something to him and giggling, and Chuck was looking down at her with interest.

"Oh, that's it," Cindy said, suddenly understanding. "It's Chuck, isn't it?"

Mollie nodded mutely, her blue eyes again filling with tears. "I was going to ask him to the dance," she said, "but it looks like Sharon's going to beat me to it." She gulped. "Listen, I can't wait around here. I don't want him to see me like this."

"Okay, shrimp," Cindy said sympathetically. "See you later." As she walked away, she reflected that she'd rather have *her* problem than Mollie's problem. At least she didn't have to live next door to the water polo team.

Mollie went through the rest of the morning in a tearful daze, but by the middle of the afternoon she was beginning to feel a little more objective about things. So she'd seen Chuck walking down the hall with Sharon Woodruff. It might mean something, and then again it might not. For all she knew, Chuck might have been merely asking her about a homework assignment. And there were lots of boys Sharon could ask to the dance; just because she was walking down the hallway with Chuck didn't mean that she was planning to ask him. Mollie gave herself firm orders: It was silly to overreact when she wasn't sure she had anything to overreact *about*.

Anyway, Mollie wasn't the kind to just sit around twiddling her thumbs. That was why she stopped at the video shop on the way home from school and rented a copy of the movie *Downhill Racer*. When Chuck and Roger had talked about skiing that afternoon at the pizzeria, Chuck had said it was one of his favorite movies. And that was why she watched from the upstairs window until she saw Chuck come home from school and then picked up the phone and dialed his number.

"Hi, Chuck," she said casually when he answered the phone. "Glad I caught you. This is Mollie."

"Oh, hi, Mollie," he said. "I just this minute walked in the door. How are you?"

"Listen, I just happened to pick up *Downhill Racer* at the video shop," she said, "and I thought I'd watch it tonight on our VCR. I know you're interested in skiing, and I thought you might want to see it, too. Would you like to come over?"

"Mmmm," Chuck said, a little reluctantly. "I don't really think—" Then he stopped. "But *Downhill Racer* is my favorite skiing movie, " he said, half to himself. He paused again. "Is seven-thirty okay?"

"Sure," Mollie said enthusiastically. "That'll be great." He hadn't sounded exactly delighted to accept her invitation, but at least he'd said yes. And that was the first step. Now the rest was up to her.

After she hung up the phone she raced to her closet and began to burrow through it madly, scattering clothes in every direction looking for something to wear that night.

Something special. Something that would make Chuck see that Mollie was the girl for him.

Chapter 10

*B*y seven that night, the Lewis house was almost empty. Cindy had gone out with Grant. Mrs. Lewis was catering a banquet at the yacht club, and Mr. Lewis was practicing with the men's glee club. Nicole was upstairs with her nose buried in a huge French novel called *Madame Bovary,* and Mollie was in the kitchen popping an enormous bowl of popcorn and feeling twittery with anticipation. Tonight was the big night. Tonight, Sharon Woodruff or no Sharon Woodruff, she was going to invite Chuck to the turnabout dance.

"How are you going to eat all that popcorn?" Nicole asked curiously as she entered the kitchen. "It looks like enough for a party. Is somebody coming over?"

Mollie whirled around, biting her lip. It wouldn't be a good idea if Nicole came downstairs while Chuck was there. It wasn't that she was afraid of the competition—it was just that she wanted Chuck all to herself, that was all.

"I thought you were upstairs reading," she said.

"I got bored." Nicole sighed. "All this resting is hard on the nerves." She sat down on a stool. She was wearing her bright blue jogging suit, and her chestnut-brown hair was pulled back in a casual wave. She stared at Mollie, raising both eyebrows. "You even *look* like a party. Somebody superspecial must be coming over."

Mollie looked down at herself. She was wearing a pair of tight black-and-white-print pants with a black tank top, black-strap high heels, a silver belt, and a half-dozen bracelets. She'd twisted her hair into a sophisticated bun over her right ear and pinned dangly pearl earrings into her ears. And she'd spent half an hour on her makeup.

"Oh, it's no big deal," she said casually, trying to downplay it so that Nicole wouldn't be interested. "Just a friend. We're going to watch *Downhill Racer*. Actually, I think it would be more boring for you than your book."

"That wonderful old Robert Redford movie?" Looking wistful, Nicole picked up a handful of popcorn and began to munch. "Listen, Mol, would you mind terribly if I came downstairs and watched it with you and your friend? I promise not to interrupt."

Mollie sighed. She'd wanted to be alone with Chuck. But she didn't want Nicole to feel left out of things—after all, she was only going to be home for a short while. So she said, "Yeah, sure."

Chuck rang the doorbell at seven-thirty on the dot, and full of anticipation, Mollie hurried to answer it. What would he think of her outfit? Would he be impressed at how sophisticated she looked?

But Chuck didn't seem impressed; he just looked startled. "Gosh," he said, glancing down at his cut-offs and sneakers and then back at Mollie, "you didn't tell me it was a formal evening."

"There's nothing formal about pants and a tank top," she said defensively, and then led him into the family room. But if she was disappointed at Chuck's reaction, she couldn't help feeling gratified when she introduced him to Nicole, who was sitting on the sofa. From the look of surprise that crossed Nicole's face, it was obvious that her sister hadn't been expecting a guy—much less a guy as good-looking as Chuck.

"Nicole can't get up to say hello," Mollie quipped, going over to turn on the VCR and the TV. "She's an invalid."

Chuck sat down on the sofa. "I thought there were only *two* Lewis girls," he said, raising his eyebrows. "Where have *you* been hiding?"

Nicole laughed. "I'm supposed to be away at Briarwood College back East. But I got sick and everybody thought it would be a good idea if I took a couple of weeks off."

"Briarwood?" Chuck asked, leaning forward eagerly. "Gosh, what a small world. Listen, do you happen to know a girl named Linda Alport? She's my cousin."

Nicole gasped. "Linda? I sure do. She's in my art history class. You're kidding! You mean she's really your cousin?"

Mollie put the popcorn on the coffee table and stood there with the remote control in her hand. "Hey, you guys, are you ready for the movie?"

"Sure she's my cousin," Chuck said, intent on Nicole's question. He took a big handful of popcorn. "In fact, all of my cousins have gone to Briarwood and my mom's sister teaches there—Dr. Martha Reynolds. Maybe you know her."

Nicole squealed. "Dr. Reynolds? I can't believe this!" She looked up at Mollie. "Mollie, can you believe this? Chuck's aunt is my English teacher! Can you believe what a small world this is?"

Mollie put her hands on her hips. "Isn't it time for the movie?" she asked.

"You know," Chuck said reminiscently, settling back on the sofa, "I haven't seen Aunt Martha for quite a few years, but she's still my favorite aunt. I remember one summer when we drove East for a vacation and ..."

He stopped and squinted up at Mollie, who was frowning down at both of them. "Did you say something, Mollie?"

"I said," Mollie repeated distinctly, "isn't it time for the movie?"

"The movie?" Chuck asked. "Oh. Oh, sure. Listen, Nicole, let's talk about this later, okay? I'd like to hear what kind of teacher Aunt Martha is."

"And I'd like to know more about Linda," Nicole replied. "She's such a good student, but she's kind of shy and—"

"If you don't mind," Mollie said stiffly, clicking the play button on the VCR remote control, "*I'd* like to watch the movie." She sat down on the other side of Chuck. Things weren't going at all the way she'd hoped they would.

"Hey, this is great," Chuck said as the movie

began. "This is a terrific film, Nicole. Have you seen it?"

Nicole nodded. "Yes," she said, "but I *love* Robert Redford. I could watch him all day."

"Fine," Mollie said in a starchy voice. "Maybe we could watch him *now,* huh?"

They watched the movie in silence, except for when Chuck pointed out some of the fine points of skiing to them. When it was over Nicole glanced at Mollie and then stood up and gave an exaggerated yawn.

"It was a great movie," she said, patting her hand over her mouth, "but I'm really beat. I think I'll go upstairs. It was nice to meet you, Chuck. See you guys later." And she quickly slipped out of the room.

Feeling grateful to Nicole for leaving them alone at last, Mollie settled back onto the sofa and got ready for a comfortable conversation with Chuck. But to her dismay, he stood up, too.

"Yeah, Mollie, I'm really glad you had the idea of renting that movie. I guess it's time for me to go."

"Wouldn't you like to have a soda or something?" Mollie asked hastily, sitting forward on the edge of the sofa. "I mean, we've hardly had a minute to talk."

"Yeah, I know," Chuck said. "But it's been a long day and I've been looking forward to my evening jog to get the kinks out." He went to the door and then turned. "Listen, it was really great meeting your sister." He grinned. "I can see that *all* of the Lewis girls are knockouts. Would you tell her that I'll drop in tomorrow sometime? I'd really like to hear more about Aunt Martha."

Mollie swallowed down the disappointment that stuck like a hot lump in the middle of her throat and followed Chuck to the door. "Yeah, I will," she said. When he had gone, she closed the door behind him and leaned against it, blinking the tears back. The evening had been an entire loss. With Nicole there, she'd hardly had a chance to talk to Chuck at all, much less ask him to the dance.

She walked upstairs slowly, her feet dragging. Nicole's door was shut, and from inside the room she could hear music playing softly.

She paused outside the door, wanting to go in and talk to her sister. But something held her back—something that made her feel upset and angry.

What was it?

Was it *jealousy*?

On Saturday morning, Nicole woke up and stretched slowly, hearing the faint sound of music from the direction of Cindy's room and the raggedly emphatic *thump-bump-thud* of Mollie doing her morning exercises. From downstairs came the enticing aroma of frying bacon. Nicole smiled and stretched again, feeling deliciously lazy. It was wonderful to be back home, even if it had taken a case of mono to get her there.

Outside in the hallway, the phone rang, followed immediately by Mollie's enthusiastic yell. "I'll get it!" Then, a minute or two later, there was a tentative knock at the door and Mollie opened it a crack and peeked in. She was wearing leotards and tights, and her head bristled with plastic pink curlers. There was some sort of weird-looking white goo smeared all over her face.

"Nicole?" she whispered. "Nicole, are you awake? The phone's for you."

"For me?" Nicole asked, swinging her legs out of bed and grabbing her robe.

Mollie thrust the phone at her through the door. "I think it's Mark," she whispered.

"Mark?" Nicole drew in her breath sharply. She and Mark had dated pretty steadily when they were in high school, and for a while she'd even thought she was in love with him. He'd certainly made no secret of the way he felt about her. But he'd started putting a lot of pressure on her to go to UCLA, where he and some of the others from her class at Vista High planned to go, and she'd pulled back, realizing that she wasn't ready for such a close relationship. The breakup had been painful. Since then they'd hardly said two words to one another.

Nicole took the phone from Mollie and pulled it through the door and into her room, where she sat on the floor with her back to the wall. "Mark?" she asked. "Hi. It's Nicole."

"Nicole, are you okay?" Mark asked gruffly. "I came home for the weekend and ran into Karen Marshall this morning, and she said you were sick."

Nicole smiled at the familiar sound of Mark's voice. It was like him to be worried about her—

actually, his constant concern was one of the things that had driven them apart. But right now, it felt pretty good to have somebody worry about her. Back at Briarwood, she pretty much had to take care of herself, and nobody else worried about how she was doing.

"Yes, I'm home for a couple of weeks," she replied, "and officially I'm sick with a case of mono. But it's not really serious. I just have to sleep a lot, that's all."

"Hey, that's good." The relief in Mark's voice was obvious. "Listen, how about if I come over this morning? I'd really like to see you."

Nicole hesitated. Seeing Mark again might create problems. After all, he'd seemed unhappy for a long time after the break, and it had been upsetting for her, too. But then again, things were different now. They'd both had time to grow up a little, get a different perspective on things. And after all, she and Mark had shared a great deal.

"I'd like to see you, too, Mark," she said honestly. "Yes. Please come over."

"Be there in a flash," he promised, and hung up.

A half hour later, Nicole and Mark were sitting out on the patio, enjoying a pitcher of orange juice and fresh croissants and laughing over something that had happened in one of Mark's classes.

"And then I realized what a stupid idiot I'd been," he said, still chuckling, "and I apologized in nothing flat. But I can't help laughing every time I think about it."

Nicole was laughing, too, but at the same time

she was marveling at how different *this* Mark was from the Mark she'd dated. Oh, he *looked* the same, with the same sweet, crooked smile and the same direct, steady gaze. And he was just as honest and upfront as he'd always been. But he seemed looser now, much less tense, much less anxious about things, much less *clutchy*. Two years ago, he'd never have been able to laugh at himself the way he was just now. He looked relaxed and happy, and he acted that way, too.

For the next half hour, the two traded anecdotes about college life and compared notes about their classes. Then Mark stood up.

"Listen," he said, "I promised my mom I'd do some errands for her this morning, so I can't stay. But I've been thinking." He leaned forward across the table and touched Nicole's cheek with his finger lightly. "What would you say to a movie tonight? We wouldn't have to stay out late or anything. I know you need to get plenty of rest. We could take in a comedy. You know what they say about laughter being the best medicine."

Nicole thought for a minute. A part of her wanted to go out with Mark, but another part of her wondered whether a date with him just now was the right thing to do. Would it lead her in a direction she wasn't ready to take? And then she remembered what her mother had said about being on vacation from decisions.

"Thanks, Mark," she said, "but I think I'd better follow the doctor's orders—at least for right now." She gave him a searching look. "Can I take a rain check?"

Mark grinned and stuck his hands in his pockets. "You've got it, lady," he said. "Just give me a call, and if I'm available, we'll do it."

Nicole giggled. For a long time she'd felt uncomfortable around Mark, knowing that he wanted so much more from her than she was ready to give. But now he seemed relaxed and easy. He'd changed remarkably.

"I will," she promised.

After they'd said good-bye and Mark had left, Nicole sat for a few minutes with her eyes closed, enjoying the warm sunshine on her face. And then she heard a whistle and opened her eyes. It was Chuck, Mollie's friend from next door.

"Oh, hi, Chuck," she said, starting to get up. "I think Mollie's upstairs. I'll go get her."

Chuck sat down in the seat Mark had vacated a few minutes before. "That's okay," he said, motioning to her to sit down. He was holding something behind his back. "Yeah, in a minute. Actually, I've come to see you."

"Me?" Nicole asked, frowning a little. What did he want?

Chuck pulled his hand out from behind his back. "I've brought you a get-well present. Something every invalid needs. It's to help relieve the itch of boredom when you have to lie around in bed all the time."

"Invalid?" Nicole said indignantly. "I'm not—" And then she laughed. Chuck was holding out a backscratcher—a funny-looking little wooden hand on a wooden stick.

"See?" Chuck demonstrated, scraping the backscratcher against his shoulder blades. "You just find the exact spot where it itches and scratch away."

"Merci," Nicole said, taking the backscratcher with another laugh. She pointed to the plate of croissants on the table. "Help yourself, Chuck."

"Thanks," Chuck said, taking one. "I think I will." He began to munch on the croissant. "Tell me what the kids at Briarwood think of Aunt Martha. Is she a good teacher?"

Nicole smiled, thinking how odd it was to think of her quiet, scholarly English teacher as somebody's Aunt Martha. "Well," she said, taking another croissant from the plate, "she has a reputation for giving really tough tests, and she's a sort of no-nonsense type in the classroom. But she's got a sense of humor, too. One time ..."

Upstairs, Mollie was just finishing her exercises, sweating under the white goo she'd plastered on her face. The week before, she'd found a terrific face cream that promised to completely do away with wrinkles. Certain that she never wanted to have wrinkles, she'd invested most of her allowance in a jar of the stuff, and this morning she'd smeared it on thickly, reasoning that the exercise might make the cream work faster and better. She wasn't sure whether it was working or not, but she *was* sure of one thing. She felt better about what had happened last night, especially since she'd intercepted Mark's phone call to Nicole this morning. Really, it was silly to be jealous of Nicole or to worry about whether Chuck liked her. After all, Nicole was in college now; Chuck was too young for her. If she was going to be interested in anybody, she'd probably be interested in Mark again.

So today, Mollie told herself, winding up the last of her twenty-five leg lifts, she would think positive. Today was the day she was going to ask Chuck to the dance. Of course, she didn't want to be too obvious about it. She'd have to come up with a scheme whereby she could just sort of bump into him casually, like out in front of the house or something, and then in an oh-by-the-way tone invite him to the dance. As she finished the very last leg lift, she felt a hollowness in the pit of her stomach and decided to finish making her plans over something to eat.

Still dressed in her old hot-pink leotard and yellow tights, with her hair full of plastic curlers and wearing the white wrinkle-cream on her face, Mollie went down the stairs and into the kitchen. Cindy was feeding Winston, and her mother was just loading the dishwasher with the last of the breakfast dishes.

Mollie went to the refrigerator. "Any orange juice?" she asked, looking around.

"Nicole made a pitcher of it and took it outside," Mrs. Lewis said. "I think she took the croissants, too. She and Mark were having breakfast together."

"Mark just left," Cindy told them, dumping a can of Winston's favorite dog food into his dish while the shaggy black dog watched, his tail thumping eagerly on the floor. "I heard his car. He asked Nicole for a date," she added, "but she said no."

"Cindy," Mrs. Lewis rebuked, "were you eaves-dropping?"

Cindy put down Winston's bowl. "The window was open," she said innocently. "I couldn't help but overhear." She went to the sink to rinse off the spoon. "I think Nicole's still outside on the patio," she added to Mollie. Then she looked at Mollie and drew back in mock horror. "What's that on your face? Are you trying out for a part in *Friday the Thirteenth*?"

Mollie ignored Cindy's insult. "Well, I guess I'll go outside and have breakfast with Nicole," she said to her mother.

Mrs. Lewis turned away from the sink. "Like that?" she asked, raising her eyebrows. "Don't you think it would be a good idea to wash your face first?"

Mollie pulled herself up in a dignified manner. "Listen, this stuff is *expensive,*" she said. "It's not something you just put on and then take off five minutes later. You have to give it plenty of time to do its thing."

Cindy chuckled. "Well, maybe you'd better try a bag over your head for the next couple of hours while it's doing its thing," she said. She looked at her watch. "Oops! Gotta get going. Bye." And with that, she dashed out the garage door.

Mollie opened the door onto the back patio and went out, carrying an empty glass for juice. The table where Nicole was having breakfast was just around the corner and Mollie called cheer-fully, "Hey, Nicole, want some company for break-fast? I've got an idea I want to try out on you about asking Chuck to the dance."

But on rounding the corner, Mollie realized to her horror that Nicole wasn't alone at the patio table. *Chuck* was with her! Just at that moment, Nicole looked up and Chuck turned around.

"Mon Dieu!" Nicole gasped, her blue eyes widening.

Looking startled, Chuck put down the croissant he was eating. "Mollie?" he asked incredulously. "Is that *you*?"

Mollie froze.

And then, with a loud screech, she dropped her glass and fled for the safety of the kitchen.

Chapter 11

*A*fter a minute, Chuck stood up. "I guess," he said, red-faced from the effort not to laugh, "I'd better go."

Nicole smothered her own smile. "Yes," she said, getting up, too, and picking up the pitcher and the empty plate. "That would probably be a good idea. I'll go talk to her. She probably feels pretty embarrassed."

Chuck laughed a little. "Well, if you want to know the truth," he said, "I am, too. I mean, I shouldn't have barged in on you guys so early. But I don't have sisters, so I don't know what girls do on Saturday mornings—or what they look like," he added with a grin.

Nicole nodded. "I can see how that would make a difference," she replied thoughtfully. Imagine being an only child, and not having any sisters. What a horrible thought. Then something else occurred to her. What had she missed by not having any brothers? Were there things that she would never know about boys simply because she'd never lived with any? What would it have been like to have a brother around to teach the Lewis girls something about boys? Even a younger brother, like Chuck? It was an intriguing thought.

Chuck went to the edge of the patio. "I'll see you later, huh? Next time, I'll bring that book for Aunt Martha."

"Sure," Nicole said. "I'll be glad to take it to her when I go back to Briarwood."

When I go back to Briarwood? she thought to herself. She stood and looked around the familiar backyard for a moment, thinking about all the great times she'd had there playing with her sisters. Briarwood, with all its problems and hassles, seemed as remote as Mount Everest—and just about as uninviting and formidable. If the decision had been up to her instead of the doctor, she never would have left school, but now that she was home, the comfort and security were almost overwhelming. The simple truth was, she *wanted* to stay.

Still thinking, she put the pitcher and the plate into the dishwasher, then went upstairs and knocked on Mollie's door.

"Go away!" Mollie's voice was tearful but emphatic.

"Don't you think we ought to talk about it, *ma chérie*?" Nicole coaxed gently. "Talking might make you feel better."

"I'd rather feel miserable than talk about it," Mollie wailed. "Go away!"

Nicole sighed. When Mollie used that oh-woe-is-me tone of voice, there was no point in trying to talk her out of it. She was just going to feel miserable until she decided to quit feeling miserable, and that's all there was to it. Nicole went to her room and lay down on the bed, still turning the Briarwood problem over in her mind. After a few minutes, she drifted off to sleep. Her last thought was that worrying about what she was going to do was as *tiring* as climbing Mount Everest!

When Mollie had gotten to her room after fleeing upstairs, she had flung herself across her unmade bed, sobbing. Now, a half hour later, she was sitting on the floor, red-eyed from crying, playing one of her favorite tapes. She'd washed off the wrinkle cream and changed into a pair of shorts and a T-shirt.

Obviously, Mollie told herself, the whole thing with Chuck was a giant catastrophe! Not only had she failed to make a good impression on him the night before when she'd been all dressed up, but she'd made a *terrible* impression on him this morning, wearing mismatched leotard and tights, her hair up in curlers, and, horror of horrors, white goo lathered all over her face. How utterly *gross*!

And not only had she missed out last night on asking him to the dance, but she might as well kiss off the possibility of asking him, period. He must have heard what she'd said out there on the patio—she'd certainly said it *loudly* enough. Thinking about it, she fell back on the floor, covering her eyes with her hands. It was horrible, that's what it was.

And then a thought occurred to her that was

even more horrible, and she sat up straight, dropping her hands, her eyes widening. What had Chuck been doing there having breakfast with Nicole? He must have come to see *her*! Did that mean that Chuck was interested in her sister, romantically interested? And could it possibly be that Nicole was interested in him? After all, Mollie remembered with a gulp, Cindy had said that Nicole turned Mark down for a date. Had she said no to Mark because she'd rather go out with Chuck instead?

Mollie doubled over and collapsed into a moaning heap on the rug.

On Sunday night Cindy was upstairs in her room, buried in her homework for the next day. Nicole was watching TV with Mr. and Mrs. Lewis in the family room, and Mollie, barefoot and wearing her old green robe, had just brought down a dirty blouse to wash so that she could wear it to school the next day. She was in the laundry room, just off the kitchen, when she heard the doorbell.

"I'll get it," Nicole called from the family room as Mollie cocked an ear. But when she didn't hear anything else, she measured soap into the washing machine and then pushed the buttons carefully, waiting to see what would happen. Once before she'd made a stupid mistake and wound up with soapsuds all over the floor.

While she waited for the machine to fill up, Mollie thought about the weekend. It had pretty much been a total bust, beginning with Friday night and climaxing with Saturday morning, and the rest of the time had been downhill from there.

She hadn't seen Chuck because she hadn't dared to step out of the house. And she'd gone out of her way to avoid talking to Nicole alone. If Nicole was interested in Chuck, Mollie didn't want to know it.

When the washer started to fill, Mollie put her blouse in, pulled her robe tighter, and started to open the louvered door. But as she pushed the door open, to her dismay she heard voices in the kitchen. Nicole's voice and *Chuck's* voice! She yanked the door shut and backed up against the washer, her hands flying to her mouth to smother a horrified shriek. She couldn't go out into the kitchen in front of Chuck looking like this! She was trapped!

"This is as good a place to talk as any," Nicole said, raising her voice over the noise of the washing machine in the adjacent laundry room. "Are you sure you don't want me to call Mollie? I think she's upstairs doing her homework."

"Actually," Chuck said, "I'd rather make this a private conversation. Okay?"

"Okay," Nicole said, a little surprised. "Well, in that case, why don't I make us some hot chocolate?"

"Sure," Chuck said. He pulled the stool up to the counter. "I hope you don't mind my coming over unannounced—again. I promise not to make a habit of it." He grinned. "Next time I'll call first."

"Don't worry about it," Nicole said. Actually, she was thinking it was nice to be comfortable enough with a boy so that you didn't mind his coming over without calling first. She got the milk out of the refrigerator and the chocolate syrup from the cupboard over the stove. "Did you bring the book for Aunt Martha?" She giggled, thinking how awful it would be if someday in class she called her English teacher "Aunt Martha." "For Dr. Reynolds, I mean."

Chuck put a book on the counter. "Yeah, here it is. Tell her I'm sorry to have kept it so long. To tell the truth," he added sheepishly, "I never did read it. It's a book of poems by Elizabeth Barrett Browning, and I hate poetry—especially love poetry. It makes me feel as if I'm eavesdropping on somebody's private life, and I don't want to."

In the laundry room, Mollie gave a choked splutter and slid down onto the floor. That was exactly the way she felt right now. She was eavesdropping on somebody's private life—Nicole's and Chuck's—and she didn't want to. But there wasn't a thing she could do about it. It was a calamity—absolutely the worst situation of her whole life!

"Oh, poetry isn't so bad," Nicole said. She stopped stirring the hot chocolate and picked the book up off the counter. "Think of it this way," she said, leafing through it. "You might get involved with a girl some time, and the poetry might come in handy. 'How do I love thee,'" she read aloud in a dramatic voice, "'let me count the ways.'"

Chuck grunted. "Getting involved with a girl would be pretty neat," he said. "If she was the right girl. But it's hard to imagine *me* spouting poetry. I'd be more likely to just tell her that I like her a lot, and to heck with counting the ways."

"The direct approach, huh?" Nicole chuckled and closed the book. "Yes, I agree. Poetry has its place, but honesty is the best policy, as far as I'm concerned." She went back to stirring the chocolate.

Chuck paused. "Speaking about approaches," he said, "I have a problem that's bothering me a little. Well, a lot, I guess. Maybe you're just the person to suggest the approach I could take."

"A problem?" Nicole asked, curious. "What kind of a problem?"

Chuck grinned ruefully. "Her name's Mollie," he said. "She's really a sweet kid, but sometimes she can be one whale of a problem."

In the laundry room, sitting on the floor, Mollie gulped and buried her flaming face in her hands. *A whale of a problem?* Was *that* what he thought about her? She felt like a worm. She felt like sticking her fingers in her ears and shutting out whatever he was going to say. But she couldn't. It hurt—it hurt horribly—but she had to hear it.

Nicole laughed a little, understanding. "Yes, Mollie *is* sweet," she agreed, "and so incredibly enthusiastic about everything. I've missed her so much while I've been away at school. Life just isn't the same without Mollie around."

"A lot quieter, I'll bet," Chick said wryly. He took a sip of his chocolate and then put his cup down. "The problem is, Nicole, that I don't feel about Mollie the way I think she'd *like* me to feel. I mean, I just don't feel romantic. I've been trying to let her know that, sort of indirectly, but ... well, she doesn't seem to get the hint."

Nicole leaned her elbows on the counter. "You know, Mollie's not exactly the indirect type herself," she mused thoughtfully. "When she wants something, she goes for it. When she feels passionate about something, she lets you know. I guess that's one of the reasons I love her so much."

Chuck reflected for a minute. "Yeah," he said finally, "I see what you mean. With a lot of people, you never know where you stand. But that's not true about Mollie. You *always* know where you stand with her."

"Well, then," Nicole said, straightening up, "doesn't that give you your clue? I mean, Mollie is really very mature. She can handle the direct approach."

"So I guess I ought to be honest and come right out and tell her how I feel, huh?"

"In my opinion, you'd be doing both you *and* Mollie a big favor," Nicole said. "She might be disappointed, but in the long run she'll be glad to know how you feel."

There was another silence. Chuck picked up a paper napkin and began to pleat it in his fingers. "Maybe I'd better be honest about something else, too, while I'm at it."

Nicole finished her chocolate and took her cup to the sink to rinse it out. "What's that?" she asked.

"It's about you," Chuck said.

Nicole turned around. He was gazing intently at her. "About me?" she asked in surprise.

"Yeah." He swallowed, then went on. "I mean, I know this is kind of soon, Nicole. And I know that you're a couple of years older than I am. But I just have to tell you that I'm really attracted to you. Do you think that maybe ..." He cleared his throat. "When you come home for the holidays, would you go out with me?"

Nicole stared at him for a minute. Then she said, as gently and honestly as she could, "Thanks a lot for the compliment, Chuck. You make me feel really flattered. Especially since I *am* older than you are."

Chuck sighed. "It sounds like you're trying to say no."

Nicole put her hand on his arm. "I'm trying to say that I value your friendship, Chuck," she said softly. "In fact, I was thinking after we talked this morning how much I've missed in life by not having a brother, somebody who could teach me what I need to know about the way guys think. But I'm not ready to take on a relationship right now—at least not a new one."

Chuck nodded and got off the stool. "Yeah. Well, I guess I understand that." His voice was gruff. "And thanks for being honest. I really appreciate it." He grinned with an effort. "And if you're serious about wanting a brother, maybe we can arrange something."

Impulsively, Nicole gave him a hug. "Thanks," she said. "I appreciate it." Suddenly, from the direction of the laundry room, she heard a sneeze. She looked up sharply and saw the door move as if somebody had nudged it.

"Was that somebody sneezing?" Chuck asked, looking around.

"I don't think so," Nicole said, steering him out into the hall. "Listen, Chuck, thanks again for coming over. I'll make sure that Elizabeth Barrett Browning finds her way back to Aunt Martha."

"Thanks for the advice," Chuck replied. He leaned forward and kissed her on the cheek. "And listen, Nicole, don't forget what I said. Any time you want some brotherly advice, you know where to come."

In the closet, Mollie sat back on the detergent box and took a deep breath. She was bitterly disappointed—and horribly embarrassed—to hear what Chuck had to say about her. But her disappointment was partially lost in her admiration for Nicole. How honest and straightforward her sister had been when Chuck told her how he felt about her! She hadn't beaten around the bush or given him any excuses or made up any lies. She'd just told him the truth—the plain, unvarnished truth—in a gentle, caring way. Her eyes filled with tears, not tears of pain but tears of admiration. What an incredibly *wonderful* sister she had!

Suddenly the door was yanked open and Nicole stood there, glaring at her. "Were you eavesdropping on that conversation?" she demanded angrily.

Without a word, Mollie jumped up and threw both her arms around her sister and hugged her tight.

Chapter 12

"*H*ey, Carey," Cindy called, "hold up a sec, will you?" She slammed the door of the family car and locked it, then hurried across the Vista High parking lot. It was crowded with Monday-morning traffic.

Carey gave her a distant look. "Hi," she said frostily. She was obviously still out of sorts about their encounter the week before.

"Listen," Cindy said breathlessly, "I just wanted to tell you what I've decided about the water polo team." She paused, but Carey didn't say anything. "I've decided," Cindy continued, "to stay with the team."

Carey stared at her, stiffening visibly. "The *water polo* team?"

"Yeah." Cindy stuck her hands into the pockets of her khaki slacks. "I'm going to tell Coach Sweeney that I'll give the swimming team my best shot, and if that isn't good enough, then she's got the right to replace me with somebody else. But she doesn't have the right to tell me what to do with my spare time." She looked down, her voice softening. "And I don't feel right about letting my friends down when they've been counting on me." She grinned a little. "And I'm sorry for being such a grump last Friday. The whole thing was beginning to get on my nerves."

Carey bit her lip. "I'm really glad to hear you say that, Cindy. But what I was trying to tell you last Friday, before you got all huffy and stamped off, was that the team's recruited another swimmer. So if you decided you had to quit, you could do it without worrying about whether we're going to go under without you."

Cindy stared at her. "Another swimmer?"

Carey squirmed uncomfortably. "Yeah. When the guys heard that you might be quitting, a couple of them talked to Liz Wright. She said that she'd like to start swimming with us." She managed a weak grin. "But they'll be tickled that you decided to stay with the team. Gosh, *two* superstars! Terrific! Maybe now we'll actually start drawing a crowd!"

Cindy shook her head, not quite sure how she felt. Liz Wright? On the water polo team?

"Hey, Mollie, hang on."

Mollie was walking through the courtyard on her way to lunch, and she turned around. Chuck was coming up behind her.

"If you've got a minute," he said, looking a little awkward, "I'd like to talk." He gestured toward a bench. "How about sitting down?"

"Okay," Mollie said, resigned. She followed him reluctantly to the bench, the red beginning to creep up into her cheeks. It was embarrassing enough, remembering the way she had looked on Saturday morning, but the embarrassment was even worse when she recalled what he had said about her on Sunday night. She sat on the bench, keeping her eyes on the ground, and waited for him to begin.

The silence lengthened, then Chuck cleared his throat and said, "I've got something to tell you, Mollie. It's about you and me. I ... I mean, it's about the way I feel about you." He stopped, his face reddening, too. "Or I guess I ought to say it's about the way I *don't* feel about you."

Suddenly Mollie was seized with an unaccountable feeling of sympathy for Chuck. She knew what was coming, and she'd had a whole night to swallow her disappointment and get ready for it. But poor Chuck—he didn't know that she knew. He must be feeling really terrible, she thought. And suddenly she didn't want him to have to feel that way.

"Listen, Chuck," she said, putting her hand on his arm. "I think I know what you're going to say."

He stared at her. "You do?" He frowned. "Wait a minute. Did Nicole talk to you?"

Mollie took a deep breath, remembering Nicole's honesty. She could never be as terrific as her sister, but the least she could do was try.

"No," she said, looking directly at him. "The fact is that I got trapped in the laundry room last night when you and Nicole came into the kitchen. I was sitting on the detergent box while you guys were talking. I heard everything."

The redness in Chuck's face washed away and

he looked pale. "Everything?" He gulped. "You're kidding."

Mollie couldn't help a tiny smile at his evident discomfort. "Nope," she said, "I'm not kidding. I didn't *want* to hear, but I couldn't help it." She leaned forward earnestly, her smile fading. "I'm really sorry that I've been a whale of a problem, Chuck. I didn't mean to be. It all started because I wanted to be helpful when you first moved in, and then ... Well, I guess I just started liking you a lot, that's all." Self-consciously, she giggled a little. "My dad says that sometimes my enthusiasm runs away with my good sense. I guess this was one of those times."

Chuck looked at her thoughtfully. "You know, Mollie," he said after a minute, "I really do like you a lot, too. Not in a romantic way," he added hastily, "more like a ... well, like a sister, I guess. Or a really good friend."

Mollie sighed contentedly. Even if things hadn't turned out the way she'd hoped, it was pretty neat to hear Chuck say that he liked her. For a second, she considered which would be better: having a sisterly relationship with him or a friendship. But that was a decision she didn't have to make just now. It was probably true what Sarah said: things like this took time. You couldn't force them.

"Well," Chuck said, standing up, "guess I'd better get some lunch." He looked at her, grinning, and cocked his head. "You hungry?"

Mollie stood up, too. "Yeah," she said, making a face, "but I hear they're serving dirtyburgers today. I guess they've maxed out on awful, huh?"

"Who cares?" Chuck asked expansively, looking down at her. He put one arm around Mollie's shoulders and held up his bookbag with the other hand. "I just happen to have a giant peanut-butter-and-banana sandwich tucked away in here. How about it, short stuff? Want half?"

"Sounds great to me," Mollie said happily, and they walked off together in the direction of the cafeteria.

That evening after school, Mollie knocked tentatively on Nicole's door.

"Come in," Nicole called from the bed, where she was sitting cross-legged. She covered the mouthpiece of the phone. "I'm talking to Mark, but don't go away, huh? I want to hear what happened with Chuck today."

Mollie sat down on a pile of pillows and relaxed. She could still feel a few pangs of disappointment when she thought about Chuck, but she had the suspicion that they'd fade pretty fast. And anyway, the cute boy in English who had smiled at her a couple of weeks ago had stopped her after class and asked her a couple of questions about their homework.

"But I guess the main thing," Nicole was saying to Mark, "is the big classes. At Briarwood, most of my classes are really small—around twenty-five or so—and I know all my teachers."

Mollie stopped thinking her own private thoughts and started listening to Nicole's conversation. Why was Nicole talking to Mark about UCLA?

After a few minutes of listening, Nicole said, "No, I'm not interested in transferring, Mark. I'm determined to make a success of my courses at

Briarwood." She smiled into the phone. "In fact, I've been feeling so healthy that the doctor says I can even catch a plane back next Sunday. And I've got all my homework caught up, too, so I can take exams next week." Another pause, and then a softer look came into her eyes. "Friday night? Yes, that would be nice. Okay. I'll see you then." And she hung up the phone.

"You're going out with Mark on Friday night?" Mollie asked with interest.

Nicole nodded. "I need a good dose of friends—and sisters, too—to fortify myself for going back to Briarwood." She looked curiously at Mollie, wondering whether her sister had been devastated by her conversation with Chuck. "Speaking of friends, what happened with you and Chuck today? Did you talk to him?"

"Yes, we talked," Mollie said happily as she sat on Nicole's bed. "I haven't decided whether I'm going to be his sister or his best friend." She gave Nicole a starry-eyed look. "Isn't it nice to be able to reveal your feelings to a boy honestly without having to worry about what you're saying or he's thinking?"

Nicole grinned and hugged Mollie. "Yes," she replied, "it's pretty wonderful. Sometimes I get the feeling that that's the way things are supposed to be, only they keep getting all mixed up." She thought for a minute. "I love my sisters," she said, "but sometimes I wish I'd had a brother. What do you think it would have been like if there'd been a boy in the family?"

"Hey, you guys," Cindy said, sticking her head around the door, "is this a private hug-fest or is there room for one more?"

Nicole scooted over on the bed and patted the space beside her invitingly. "Always room for one more," she said. "Did you talk to Coach Sweeney this afternoon? What did she say when you told her you were staying with the water polo team? Was she mad?"

With a big grin on her face, Cindy sat down on the bed. "She threw up her hands and said, 'Well, I guess I can't fight city hall.'"

"City hall?" Mollie asked in a mystified tone. "Why on earth would a coach want to fight city hall?"

"Liz Wright is joining the water polo team," Cindy explained. "And that makes two of us. So I guess Coach Sweeney feels outnumbered. Anyway, she's backing off." A big grin crossed her face. "And today I beat Liz Wright in *two* timed trials." She reached for Nicole and squeezed her hand. "Thanks a bunch for your advice, sis."

Nicole laughed. "I have the feeling you didn't need it," she said. "Sounds as if you solved your problem all by yourself."

"Maybe," Cindy replied with a grin. "But with Liz on the water polo team, things are just beginning to get interesting." She looked at Mollie. "Did you and Chuck get things settled, shrimp?"

"Uh-huh," Mollie said, looking thoughtful. Suddenly an idea struck her and her eyes gleamed excitedly. "Hey," she said, "I've just got this terrific idea! How would you guys feel if we named Chuck an honorary Lewis?"

Cindy raised both eyebrows. "An honorary Lewis?"

"Sure," Mollie said happily. "Nicole and I were

just saying how neat it would be if we had a brother in the family. Well, there's this terrific guy next door who would make a marvelous brother." As she talked, her excitement grew. "So why don't we fix up some adoption papers and decorate the living room and get Mom to give us some stuff to eat and have an adoption party?" She paused, out of breath, and looked expectantly from Cindy to Nicole. "Well?" she demanded. "What do you think? Isn't it a great idea? Isn't it an absolutely *outrageous* idea?"

Cindy looked at Nicole. "Do you know what *I* think?" she asked meaningfully.

Nicole looked at Cindy. "I bet I can guess," she said. They each picked up a pillow.

Hastily, Mollie got off the bed and began to back away. "Listen, you guys," she said, holding up her hands, "maybe it wasn't such a good idea after all. Maybe—*help!*" she shrieked as Cindy pounced on her with the pillow.

For the next few minutes, the air was filled with giggles and yelps and laughs, as the three Lewis sisters tickled and pummeled and pounded one another with pillows. Afterward, they sprawled helplessly on the floor, exhausted with laughter.

"On second thought," Mollie gasped, "I don't think there's *room* in my life for a brother—not with you two guys taking up so much space."

Cindy smothered a last giggle. "Yeah," she said, "with the three of us as sisters, the poor guy wouldn't have a chance, would he, Nicole?"

Nicole looked at the two of them and smiled. "Not a chance in the world," she said contentedly.

Here's a sample of what awaits you in CAMPUS FEVER, book sixteen in the "Sisters" series for GIRLS ONLY.

Mr. Lewis had tilted his chair back and was listening to the conversation with the most peculiarly self-satisfied expression on his face. Mollie planted her elbows on the table and looked at him squarely. "Daddy, why do I have the distinct impression that you know something about Nicole that we don't."

Richard Lewis leaned toward Mollie and affectionately pinched her cheek. "Because, little one, you are a good detective."

"You've heard from Nicole?" Mrs. Lewis said, astonished. "She is okay, isn't she?"

"She was this afternoon," he hastened to assure his wife. "Not that she bothered to call me!" he said with a sniff. "I called her." He stopped just long enough to get Mollie squirming in her seat, then laughed. "You see, I have to go to Boston Monday on business."

The girls' faces fell.

"Oh, Richard, not another business trip?" Mrs. Lewis sounded crestfallen.

"But Boston's not far from Nicole's school!" Cindy said slowly, then grinned at her father. "You'll get to see her." Cindy clapped her hands together. "Awesome! Nicole must have flipped out when she heard."

"A little!" Cindy's dad admitted.

"I can hear her now!" Mollie jumped up and tilted her head in the air. *"Quelle chance! Papa. Merveilleux!"* Mollie's imitation of her big sister's habit of saying every other word in French cracked everyone up.

"She was pleased," Mr. Lewis said slowly, "but not half as happy as when I told her the rest of my news."

He reached into his jacket pocket and withdrew a long narrow envelope. He turned to his wife. "This is one business trip that won't bother you at all. In fact, I can't think of anyone at this table not being absolutely delighted—unless, of course, they have plans for next weekend."

"Next weekend?" Grant asked, and looked sharply at Cindy. Cindy didn't notice. Her eyes were fixed on her father. She looked at the envelope and suddenly let out a whoop.

"Those are plane tickets and—"

Mollie finished for Cindy. "And we're all going with you!" She flopped down on the bench in a mock faint, then instantly popped up again and exclaimed, "What'll I wear? I'd better start packing right away."

"Whoa!" Mr. Lewis gestured for the girls to calm down. "We don't leave until Friday, and we're there for Briarwood's Homecoming Weekend. I thought, because of the business trip and all, I might as well spring for it. It seemed the perfect thing to cheer up Nicole, and besides, neither of you girls have seen the college yet."

"I don't believe this!" Cindy let out a happy laugh. "I'm getting to go to Massachusetts in the fall, visit a real ivy-league college, and see Nicole. This must be a dream!"

Mollie just jumped up and hugged her father.

Mr. Lewis put his arm around his youngest daughter and looked around the table. "Of course, if any of you have other plans . . ." he teased.

"Other plans?" Mollie stared at her father as if he had suggested she start dating a boy from Mars.

"Wild horses couldn't keep me from going on this trip to see Nicole!" Cindy enthused. She turned to Grant, all smiles.

He stood up and looked down at her with the most peculiar expression. Cindy's smile suddenly felt very wrong. "Grant?" She started to ask him what was wrong, but her voice came out funny. He didn't seem to hear.

Without looking at her, he said, "I've got to get going." Running the words all together he mumbled in Mrs. Lewis's direction, "thankyoufordinner." Then he hurried across the lawn toward his bike.

"What's with him?" Mollie said as Grant vanished down the road toward the beach.

Cindy slowly shook her head, then got up. "Nothing a couple of brownies can't clear up!" she said, grabbing a handful from the plate and starting to follow him. But her voice sounded shaky and, to Mollie's ears, a little scared.